D1120713

China Blue

© 2021 Catherine Gammon

With occasional variations, some individual chapters have
appeared previously in the following publications: "Night Vision"
in *The Missouri Review*, "Facing North" in *Fiction International*, "Earth
Tides" in *The Agni Review*, and "Mama's Night of Dreams" in
Shankpainter.

Published by Bridge Eight Press
Jacksonville, Florida

All rights reserved.

www.bridgeeight.com

ISBN 9781087901718
LCCN 2020942889

Printed in the USA
Cover & book design by Jared Rypkema

In memory

With gratitude for their friendship
during my years in Provincetown

R. D. Skillings (1937-2020)
Denis Johnson (1949-2017)

China Blue

China Blue

Night Vision

It is early when we go into my room, seven maybe, or eight. In February it's already dark. I have turned the lights off in the kitchen, the front room. China Blue is standing by my bed, dropping his shoes.

In the beginning we stood with our clothes on, lay down wearing clothes, felt the other's body through clothes. Now we undress immediately.

Get me to bed quick, he says. Before I change my mind.

I don't want to spin a lot of fancy images, I'm not a razzler-dazzler. I don't want to deviate from the real, don't want to stray into what is not, what might be, or what I fear or wish were true. I want to be accurate. I want to direct a narrow, focused beam onto his face, into his eyes, and undress his mind. But it can't be caught that way. He talks reluctantly, easily only in bed, between one fuck and another, our arms and legs entwined. Every night we spend together is the first again, and the last. I have to strip him down obliquely. He vanishes with the day.

One Saturday in December, very cold, I was walking early in the center of town when a woman crossed Commercial Street in front of me. She was wearing a bright gold robe that hung unevenly from under her sealskin coat. It looked like a bedspread. Her legs were bare and she was wearing rubber thongs. She was beautiful. I wanted to know everything about her: why she would be walking so early on such a cold morning with bare feet. She turned around and asked me if I knew the time. Before nine, I said, I don't know exactly. She nodded. She was very beautiful. She must have been drinking. I wanted to be that free. That beautiful and destroyed. She was an image my mother once had of herself. For years Mama believed she would die in the gutter at twenty-five. When she didn't, she became a survivor. But this barefooted woman just keeps on dying. Her smile was glorious. I don't think she's any younger than my mother is. I see her now, on the streets, in bar windows, I see her everywhere. Three days later, I spent my first night with China Blue.

Mama needs a fix. She's addicted to his body, to his long-fingered hands, to his skin. She's addicted to his precise, quiet voice saying, *Turn around, I was hoping you would do that, Do you want me to get on top?* She's addicted to his semen, which she swallows, to the pulse that ripples up his cock against her tongue before he comes.

Am I hurting you? he wants to know.

Are you in the habit of hurting people?

No, he says.

Because I was moving your fingers away?

Yes.

I didn't want you to do that now.

What do you want?

2

I want you.

You want me how?

Inside me.

Just my cock inside you.

Yes, she tells him. Yes.

In the mirror of her window at night she studies her face. She holds her hair back from her forehead with her hands. She wishes she could see the image clearly when she takes her glasses off. Without her glasses what she sees is a wash of pale skin, a purple robe, black night, an impressionist sketch, the asparagus fern in the window blurring green and bright out of the darkness. She pulls her glasses down again. In the lenses the lamplight is reflected. The frames are dark, amber plastic, and they break up her face. Her hair hangs around her temples, too long to be bangs, too short to stay off her eyes. Her eyes look dark tonight. Her earring catches a glint from the lamplight. She has a high forehead when she pulls her hair back. Her mouth is full. Her neck is bare. Her robe hangs open. She is waiting for him, but we both know tonight he will not come. She watches herself in the window. She knows she is not beautiful. But sometimes, if she looks at herself long enough, she thinks she has never seen another woman as beautiful as that image there in the glass.

When situations are undefined, anything that happens becomes the definition. Sometimes the cat smells like sour milk. Mama remembers baby diapers. China Blue is so inaccessible he drives us to invent. They grow inarticulate together. She has known men who change with the moon, but this one turns at midnight. Catch

3

him before or after, she says, and pay attention to the time.

When they first step into her room, they're blind in the darkness. Only the sound tells her he's taking off his shoes. After a while, separately, they realize they've begun to see. In the quiet between sex they are able to talk. He asks what her father is like. She tells him. She tells him how he died. China Blue counts his children, who've never been born. I am thirteen. I embroider peace signs, yin/yang signs, Scorpio signs, *I Love the Beatles, Disco Sucks*, and shooting stars and rainbows all over my jean jacket. I wear my yellow hair loose and long, and collect unicorns. In the summers, I visit my father. My mother's hair used to be as long as mine is. Now it's shorter than China Blue's. She walked out after him one night in January, with bare feet on frozen snow, then came back in and began to cut. She can't stop cutting. Every day I find new trimmings in the wastebasket, hair ends clinging to the wet porcelain sink.

I ask China Blue if that's really his name.

My father was a sailor, he says. There was a family fortune somewhere. Then he took up aviation and began to scatter the wealth. He laughs.

We lie in my bed like spoons.

Since Mama started cutting her hair, pictures fall from the walls, objects suddenly break, fuses blow. She went across the street one night to have dinner with Mason. When she got there, he was changing a lightbulb, and as he screwed it into the socket, the house went dark. One afternoon the radio fell off the refrigerator when neither of us was near. Something broke inside it. Now Mama can only hear the news by sitting close to the speaker, when there's no sound anywhere else in the room. In our kitchen a purple and blue and silver pinwheel attached to the corner of an upper cupboard keeps us from bumping our heads. The pinwheel comes down now, every day. We hear it sometimes, falling into a silence with a clack and whish across the floor, in the morning before we get up, or late at night, when we're all quiet, or after China Blue's gone home. Mama says it's her poltergeist. At a party she felt she could spontaneously combust.

You have a poltergeist? he asks her in a bar when she's describing her new radius of chaos to their friends.

Yes, she tells him. But it's mine. Mine, Mama says, knowing what he is thinking. Mine, not hers.

China Blue has fantasies he never tells my mother. He hides with me in the night.

I burn the kitchen trashcan when Mama's across the street, talking and drinking with Mason. When she leaves I'm lying in bed drawing the head of a unicorn in black charcoal. The unicorn is facing me. The longer I work on it the darker it gets, and after a while I know I have to burn it. It's torn in four pieces. I hold them into the flame of a black candle I light at the stove, and when almost nothing's left, I drop the corners into the trash. I thought they were done burning, but from my room I smell garbage and rubber, and I'm back in the kitchen, looking at fire, when the smoke alarm above the table goes off. The air is floating with ash. The sound scares me. It's loud and insisting, and tattoos like a high-speed amplified drum. It goes off sometimes when we're cooking, and

Mama talks to it while she opens the door and a window to shut it up. Not *now*, she says. Or, Stupid, it's only fried fish, can't you tell fried fish yet? It stops and starts as fresh air gusts in. She keeps talking to it, pausing to listen, as if they are having a conversation. I put the fire out quickly with an old pair of pants that don't fit and water, and no damage is done except to the trashcan. Then I open the door and windows to get the alarm to stop. The kitchen is tiny. Ashes are everywhere, the rubber trashcan a gnarled mess. In a few places it's burned through to the yellow floor. I pry the hard, melted rubber up with a knife and take the trashcan outside to the garbage bins. I don't want Mama to see. I have to leave her a note. First I clean the kitchen, wondering how much I can say. I don't want her to lecture me about playing with fire, because I wasn't playing. I don't like to think about it, because the fire was scary and stupid, and because I had to burn that drawing. I don't want to have to explain to her. But I do have to and I leave her a note. I try to tell her how Jane and Rainy and me were talking about black and white, because Rainy has a friend she thinks is turning black. What I drew was dealing with this, but I didn't realize it till after drawing it, so I tore it up because I don't want to be involved. But after talking to Jane on the phone I decided to burn it, since throwing it away wasn't really destroying it. Then I ask Mama please not to bring it up, I don't really want to talk about it because I'm not involved with all that black and white stuff, I burned the drawing because I don't want to be involved, and I can't talk about what I don't know. It's a silly note, full of *pleeze* and *cuz* and *kinda*, and I know she'll come in and wake me anyway. While I'm waiting, I think about China Blue. I think about how he'd understand this: the black and the white, the unicorn, the

6

fire. I think he already knows, as if he's been here, watching, even though the reason Mama's at Mason's, talking and talking, is that China Blue's not coming tonight. I sleep a little until I hear her. I've left the ceiling light on, the note on the table, I listen while she reads it. She comes into my room in the dark. She doesn't lecture me about the fire. I don't know why I thought she would. She never lectures me that way. She wants to know about the drawing, she wants to know about the black and the white. She's on every left list in the country and since the last election she always talks about the Klan, neo-Nazis, fascism spreading suddenly, rapidly, all through the world. She knows what this town can be like, how too many people are narrowly bred here and full of hate. She thinks I'm going to tell her this *black and white stuff* is some kind of racist talk, moving through the school, through the streets. At the end of summer at a churchyard flea market she found a table where a man was selling brass KKK buckles. There was a crateload of them, along with crates of glove hands, shoe feet, and other odd things in multiple quantity. The Klan buckles made her angry and she wanted to go into the church to complain. But she didn't go. There's no law against it, she said. But she was furious and left the flea market right away. Now she thinks I'm going to tell her the Klan is here, in town recruiting kids. I know it isn't funny, but I have to laugh at her.

How could Rainy have a friend *turning black?* I say.

Lots of ways, she says. If it's not that, what is it?

I tell her it's about good and evil. The more white you are, the more the black comes after you. I don't really understand it, which is why I don't want to talk about it. But Rainy's worried about her friend. They think the black is getting him. And my drawing was getting blacker and blacker. It was a drawing of him. I'm white. Except I'm not really involved in any of it. But the whiter you are, the faster the black comes looking for you.

Oh, it's magic, Mama says. She sounds relieved. You can talk to me about magic, she says. I know about magic.

You do?

Sure, she says. In the sixties. It came in with drugs and the Beatles. Just like for you. I can smell her whiskey breath. I wonder if she talked to Mason about China Blue. Magic is powerful, she says. It can ruin things. But it's never more powerful than you.

I don't want to be involved in it, I say. It scared me. I didn't even know what I was doing.

Its only power is the power you give it, Mama says. If you don't give it power, it doesn't have any. It can't get you. You don't have to stay away from it and you don't have to submit. You don't have to be afraid of it, either way. It's not outside you. Leave it alone if you want to. Just remember, it gets its power from you. Her voice is getting sleepy, impatient. She's preaching. She has answers. She wants to save me. She's like her father, she told China Blue. Trust me, she's saying, tell me about magic, I know a thing or two. She begins to repeat herself, sitting on the floor, her head down on the sheet beside my pillow.

Just don't bring it up again, I ask her. Please? Okay?

His skin is smooth and hairless. Nothing's between me and his body. He's almost as old as Mama but his flesh feels as young as mine. Mama seems young too, but she isn't, she's wise. China Blue is just a boy beside her. He's tall, though, and she likes that. She likes his pale skin, his dark hair, soft under her fingers. She lies against his back and runs her hand down his head, his neck, she pets him like a cat. Then she stops suddenly, afraid to claim him. She scared him the first night they spent together: she wants him too much and all the time.

Don't stop, he says. Keep doing that.

Don't look, he says in my room. I'm invisible. If you see me in here, shut those eyes.

Wandering floes, washed in from the Atlantic, trapped in the spiraling Cape tip, mass in the harbor for weeks. The bay freezes. Boats can't move. The sun comes out. At low tide the floes rise up from the sand. From Mama's window they look white and green. We walk in canyons of ice. They stand taller than our heads. When the tide comes in, they bob and drift, carried so fast finally they seem to skim the surface of the water. Within a week we're in February summer, the sun is warm, temperatures climb to the sixties. Mama takes her jacket off and walks bare-armed in the morning to the restaurant where she works. For a few days, almost everyone is happy. Mama sees Rainy in the window of the Governor Bradford, a bar where people collecting welfare, disability, or unemployment hang out, drink, play pinball, video games, backgammon, chess, and pool. Jane lives with her father now. He's a carpenter and boatbuilder and his hair falls curling almost to his ass. He hangs out at the Surf Club, where winter people working go. Mama's working hard again for a while because the sunny weather and school vacations bring tourists back to town. In the nights she waits for China Blue. In bed with him, she laughs. He makes her happy. They are quiet together, except when they're making love.

What? he asks her when she laughs.

I just remembered something, she tells him. Her right hand's first two fingers are resting in his left hand's palm. She tells him how when I was little, just beginning to walk and for a long time after, I had to hold just those two fingers—never one, never three, not two other fingers, not a whole hand.

She ritualized it, Mama says. Then she's quiet again, then she laughs. What a funny thing to remember.

It's nice, he says. It's nice to have things like that to remember.

It's dark, he whispers to me. Where are you?

Here, I say, and he stands me up against the wall and touches the nubs of new breasts through my t-shirt. My mouth tastes like toothpaste.

Yours tastes like tobacco, I say. He's pressing against me, holding my shoulders, my hips. I feel the strange shapes of him through our clothes. It frightens me, how big he is. His hands are gentle. He holds my head, my hair. He moves his fingers. I can't stand up. I plop when I hit the sheets. The night is so quiet I can only hear my breathing. China Blue is gone.

Jane and Rainy and I are talking. We're down on the wharf. All the ice has melted, or gone back to the sea. Two nights ago the moon was full. The tide is in and very high. The water's green and rises in waves, like the ocean. A storm is coming. I tell them about China Blue. I tell how he comes to my room in the night. I tell how he touches me. I tell them and tell them. I don't know why. Seagulls are screaming. Jane is fourteen and Rainy is fifteen. I want them to put him in order for me. I want them to help me to see.

On Sundays Mama and China Blue sit around drinking coffee together, reading *The New York Times*. They laugh at words and phrases made current by Alexander Haig: campaign of disinformation, augmentees, the USG. They worry that El Salvador will be the new Vietnam. Historical reality, Mama says, is not on our side. But the world of war and politics is not their true province. Between them on the table oranges are piled in a white, gleaming bowl. Their skins glow, so intense in the bright sun they hurt my eyes. The days grow longer. Mama plays poker on Tuesday nights. China Blue comes to her more often. They walk. They talk. They drive. They are seen together in the light. I like it here, he says in her bed, you can hear the foghorns, and when he says You *feel* good, resting while they're fucking, his cock still hard and deep inside her, she answers I *know* it and they go on making love. Only I stay blind to him and take him in the dark. In my room, our eyes do not become accustomed to the night. Still, it's me he comes to, me he seeks, and in the mornings, when he's gone again, and alone, when he lies wherever he lies, on beach sand, in the dunes, on his bed, staring at the ceiling, smoking, listening to birds, resisting the day, I'm the one he imagines, I'm the one he dreams.

I have learned, Mama tells me. Mind lives in what it touches, but it devours what it sees.

China Blue drives a cab, or tends bar, or waits expensive tables in the summer. Sometimes he's on unemployment. He hangs out in winter, like everyone else in this town, and works when he has to. He has dedicated his life to some purpose. What it is, he'll never say. If you ask him, he'll laugh and tell you all he wants is to live in a cabin somewhere, with a dog maybe, or any other silly thing that comes into his head. Mama's jealous. From small evidence she constructs whole worlds. She is jealous of every woman he talks to. She is jealous of his fantasies. She is jealous of him with everyone but me. She wants to know his secrets. She wants him every night. She sits at her window, studying her image. From my bedroom, tapes are playing, and sitting in her chair she dances with herself in the glass. She unbuttons her blouse, pushes her lips to a pout. She thinks he's coming, even though she's left some party or dinner or restaurant or bar before him. Why? she hopes he'll ask her. Why did you leave? And she has her answer ready: To say no to you, to avoid asking you, to avoid hearing you say no to me. If I didn't love her I would laugh. If I didn't know that what she is today I'll someday—twenty years from now—have to be.

Someone's hung the pinwheel right side up instead of upside down, and it's stopped falling. We don't know who turned it, Mason maybe, but nothing's breaking anymore, no fuses blow. Everything gets calm. Mail comes in from liberal organizations all across the country, and Mama says she bets the same computer that sells her name and address to ERAmerica, the Poverty Law Center, and Greenpeace is selling Right-to-Lifers to the Moral Majority and the Klan. She glances through the letters and saves the return envelopes. She pushpins them with their pledge cards to her bedroom door, and sometimes, when her tips are good, she takes one down and gives ten dollars. Some she throws away. When the Stop-the-Slaughter letter comes, she gives it and the pledge envelope and protest postcards to me. I want Jane and Rainy to help me donate. I show them the pictures of the harp seals, and read to them how the hunters will sweep across Newfoundland ice floes, clubbing and skinning 100,000 white-furred babies while the mothers bellow and bark.

It's a warm misty evening and I see that December woman, roller skating, spaced out on the street. Her eyes more ruined than ever, the lids hang heavy, make slits. Her shirt is pink, her pants and jacket black. Even her skates are black. She glides toward me slowly, like rowing. I think she knows who I am. She doesn't look at me when we pass. I think she knows what I see.

Mama's out with China Blue somewhere and he drops her off. She comes in and drinks half a bottle of wine in fifteen minutes and cries the rest of the night, talking to herself, to him, in the mirror where she cuts her hair. If he had a phone, she'd call him. But he doesn't, and her anger's bigger than wires.

I close my eyes and see lavender, and when I say the word to myself in my mind, I feel *lavender* move up my body—*lavender*, I don't know if it's cool or it's hot—*lavender*, I don't know if it's on the surface or under the skin—*lavender*, I don't know whether it's real, or just dreamed up out of some song.

You'd better look at him, Rainy tells me. You better look, is all. It could be anyone. Anything. Why should it be China Blue?

Doesn't he love your mother? Jane asks.

No, I say. I don't think so. I don't think he even loves me.

Someday, Mama says, I'm going to get mad at him. But not yet. He throws me into a certain kind of stillness. He's very good for me. The cat is on her lap, letting her stroke him. His hair is long and striped and orange. He has a broad, intelligent face, and big feet. He's a Maine coon. They used to be seagoing cats. At midnight he prowls the beach. His eyes are gold. He likes rain, and understands whatever he sees. Mama makes fists at her image. Through the thin skin of the backs of her hands the veins show blue, the color of her blouse, her eyes. This failure of knowledge is necessary, she says. What it can penetrate, what it gets into, mind consumes. She's playing poker tonight and tonight she's going to win. She'll take the table out for a drink and they'll stay in the bar until closing, when December Woman, wearing red, will be standing behind the counter, backed up against the bottles, her eyes wide open like nobody's ever seen them—black and blind and staring, the panic radiating out from them holding twenty people at bay. The bartender's telling the crowd to leave and calling the police, and Mama, standing closer than anyone, watches that woman's eyes.

The police? Mama says. We can't let them call the police.

Look at those eyes, says Mason. You don't interfere with eyes like that.

But look at her, Mama's saying, Look at her! and China Blue is standing in the darkness by my bed, dropping his shoes.

Facing North

He has not used his true name in years. He almost doesn't remember it. A boat is lost at sea and my father is on it. Once you had a cat. It ran off, disappeared, and your mother thought it must have died—run over, or killed in the woods by another animal. You knew the cat would come back, and after three months, it did, wild, climbing the screen door, hair tangled and matted, all teeth and claws. His mother took the cat to the vet and had it castrated. The cat calmed down. China Blue. One name. One body. Only me here. Mind busy, body idle. Every voice your own. A few days ago my brother came home. You are a sole surviving son. His brother is dead. He died in Vietnam.

His room has glass sliding doors on two sides, to the west and the north. If he leaves his heavy curtains open, light wakes him before dawn and he lies there in bed, head in his crooked elbow, looking down the length of the room and out the glass wall. On clear days you can see Pilgrim I, out the west windows, twenty-seven miles across the bay, spewing coolant steam. You dream its explosion, see mushroom clouds, yourself, your friends, your lovers, eating hot dogs on the beach, sprawled on blankets, everyone paired except you. Then he is running. Over the next dune and the next. The reactor explodes, like a bomb, but it starts in the ground and rises, shooting flames, takes that implausible form, mushrooming into the sky. It is not Pilgrim I that you see from your window but the oil-fed generator at Sagamore. Your view is southwest and northwest. You choose to forget this. This town is almost an island. The only road out runs up-Cape, south then west toward the mainland. There is no way to evacuate. Except by water or air. Swim east, they joke. I think I should buy a boat. It is still winter. We are surrounded by water. The light is high, even when the sky is gray. Light is everywhere. I am waiting for something impossible to happen.

He has no immediate neighbors. He lives off a back road. A few turns away the houses are crowded together. But here there are only the trees, cobwebbing into the sky. You feel yourself withdrawing from something. You aren't depressed or unhappy, but sometimes impatient. You have stripped the pictures from your walls, the photographs of friends, of lovers, of old men and beautiful women, the posters from the Soviet modernist collection you saw in Chicago, from the Matisse exhibition in New York, the postcards from your dead brother, the plexiglass-framed correspondence that documents your history with the Post Office and the CIA. He has taken all this down and on the longest cleared wall, the south one, above him, behind the bed, he has pushpinned an AP photo clipped from *The New York Times*. He looks at it every day. The Reverend Daniel Berrigan is wearing a cap. Something unrecognizable sticks out from his mouth, a cigarette maybe, a cigar stub, a piece of gum, a tongue depressor, or maybe it's just his tongue. Philip Berrigan (but the caption says Patrick) is talking for a microphone, chin up, eyes cast high, as if witnessing things at a distance. There is a look of good humor in their faces. They are standing outside the courthouse in Norristown, Pennsylvania. They are on the way in. In a few days they will be convicted of burglary, criminal mischief, and criminal conspiracy. With six others, also found guilty, they broke into a General Electric plant, hammered two missile nose cones, and poured blood on company papers. You wonder about the blood: what kind it was, how much they used, where they got it. From the south wall, Daniel looks west, toward Pilgrim I, and Philip, white-haired and eyes raised, is facing north. These men are brothers. They have chosen to go to prison. Their faces are beautiful. You love them. They almost make you cry.

A woman comes out of a gale, who won't say she loves you. He has spent the evening with her, drinking and talking. They had a good time. Then he left her, and she was unhappy. She walks through the gale. She taps at his glass, standing on his balcony in the wind and the rain. He gets out of bed in the dark and pulls on his jeans. She is dripping wet. He gives her a towel and she takes off her clothes. He holds her against his body in bed. Her body is ice. She tells him he's burning. They make love, because she is there. This evening, for the fourth time, he's told her they can't become lovers. It's the seventh night they've made love. Now I'm confused, he says. She says, We shouldn't have been making love again. He says, I'm too practical. They go to sleep, and in the morning he says, No one has ever walked through a gale for me before, and drives her home.

The sky is parchment, vellum. As if the light is behind it. In my ears, Elvis Costello. White knuckles. Black-and-blue skin. A stuck record, over and over, and to get rid of it I have to play the

17

tape. I lie in bed, listening. The sky gets higher. I am afraid of that woman. She does not love me. She does not.

His walls are white. The curtains red. The sky is pale, gray, silver. The light reflects back from the water. The trees are dense and bare. Their branches are threads, brown silk. Nothing changes. I wait for anything to seem do-able. He does not know why he has been so withdrawn all his life. It is not because his father died at sea. He was withdrawn before that. It was not his brother, his sister, his mother. It was that stinking narrow town that I grew up in. And I was not withdrawn all my life, only half of it, or a little more. Withdrawn until I left there. All over that high school, I had places where I hid. On television some Republican says, Every single time these people talk, millions end up enslaved by Communism. You wonder what people he means, who have such power in their words. Your walls irritate you. They are not bare enough. The shelf of books beyond your feet takes up too much space. You stare at the spines. They flatten to blocks and stripes of color. You want to take that canvas down. You turn onto your side again, curling your knees up to your chest and facing the north window, the glass door at the top of the red brick stairs. You ought to be in Gloucester, taking care of your mother. Maybe she's dead. No one knows where he is. He's been hiding for years, becoming somebody else.

His room is too crowded. In my head, the Jefferson Airplane. In my head, Mick Jagger. She said she is three people: herself, first child, survivor; her brother, a year and a half younger, born dead; her sister, three years younger, alive only fourteen hours. He stroked her damp head and asked which one of her walked through the gale. In my ears, Elvis Costello: walking on the water, no miracle man. He gets out of bed. He kicks the silent tape machine and hurts his toe. He leans on the sliding door, spread-eagle against the glass. The glass is cold. The sky is as pale as his naked skin. His toe begins to throb. He looks at his feet. Blood dots the slate floor, drying, ruby on gray. He goes back to bed. I have to get rid of things. Start with the tape player. And the bricks and boards. And all the books. The television. Then? The dresser, clothes. The table, chairs, lamps, rugs, modular foam couch. It's all too much in this little room. Too much. You lie on your back, hands under your head. You stare at the ceiling. You were a painter once. Until they lost your crate. *Lost.* No. *Confiscated.* He built a box for seven large paintings and sent them to an art school in Italy, and four months later when he hadn't heard from the program, when he inquired and finally understood his application had been incomplete because his work had never arrived, he put a tracer on the crate through the Post Office and went home to Gloucester to wait. You no longer remember your paintings, what they looked like, how they felt. They have no colors in your memory, no textures, shapes, content, form. They do not exist. You remember only the shreds, the remains of their deliberate destruction. His name then, the true one, resembled the name of a man under suspicion, already guilty of making public secret documents. After two years the crate turned up in a Washington warehouse belonging to the CIA, and when you asked for it they let it go. Your canvases were slashed— with razors or scissors or very sharp knives. The stretcher bars were sawed and broken. You sat on your mother's porch in the sun where you'd opened the crate and you stared at the mutilated paintings until after a while you stood up and you walked away.

The light turns acid, corrosive. It empties the room of its

objects. Books are gone, television's gone, couch, rug, chairs. Nothing is left here. You had a dream this color once. You rode a cable car up a hill in San Francisco, except it wasn't a real hill, not really San Francisco, but a museum, some monumental reconstruction. The light was colorless, unearthly. At the top of the hill the cable car vanished, and your fellow passengers. You were alone in a terrace garden with a parquet floor. A white wrought-iron table and chairs stood off to your right, beside the white railing. A woman appeared, a giant. You were the height of a child beside her. She stood at your left. She wore a long gray dress, very plain, her hair pulled up on her head. She was majestic, looked Victorian, felt Greek. She led you to the rail and swept her left arm slowly from horizon to horizon, as if to say *all this is yours*. You looked down. A city lay spread out below you—like San Francisco, but not San Francisco—surrounded by water. The light off skyscraper glass and rippling the water dazzled your eyes, and you raised your head and watched a planet come, transiting, turning. It was large and close enough that you recognized continents. It was Earth, so real you wondered where in time and space you stood. The planet flew by, its days passing while it turned, and slowly the dream ended, you standing there next to the woman, and even after you woke you kept asking *where?—where?*

The room is empty except for his bed and a pile of newspapers, Sunday magazines. One by one he's removed things to the basement, storing them compactly in the corner beyond the washer and dryer. In a few months, when it's time to move, he'll carry them up again. His landlord will never know—he lives in New York during winter, comes to his house only on weekends, in summer, when he rents this studio room to beautiful gay boys. You stare at the ceiling. You used to smoke, but now you don't. You have no reason to go out. Maybe for unemployment. He doesn't know what day it is. He turns his back to the room and looks at the Berrigans. The picture begins to depress him, Philip's deep cheerfulness, Daniel's eyebrows, that inexplicable thing sticking out of his mouth. These men are brothers. You want to be them. I want my brother. He does not remember his brother. He only remembers him dead. My brother's come back to me, in a crate with my dead paintings, out of a gale in the ice flesh of that woman. He rolls away, curled into himself, head between his elbows, peering out across the room. The sky has no color. It's nothing, not there. That woman has a daughter. He has desired her. He has touched her. But he won't remember. He refuses. He can dream her, her newness, like all the girls he hungered after when he went to that high school and hid. Her smallness, her firmness, her distance, like the paper girls he's torn down from his walls, the paper women he saved for their taut bellies, string bikinis, gold skin, women's bodies he's ravished now, burned, to make way for the Berrigan brothers, Alexander Haig, priests, demonstrations, soldiers, and three dead Salvadorans half-covered by a red banner crying out for UNIDAD. The figures on the priests' robes are Indian, the flags Spanish, the arms Russian, US, Israeli, Chinese. The government soldiers are boys in green. They flirt with the camera like New York models. The one standing nearest butts his rifle up from his groin, left knee slightly raised, right hand holding the weapon in a grip that looks equally firm and light. His mouth is almost smiling. His dark eyes, suggestive, showing clear whites, challenge the lens: *Want my gun, you men, you women. Come touch this five-foot erection.* The soldier beside him, a little beyond, faces the camera, legs bent and spread, balanced, rifle lowered, head lowered, whole body ready to rise, fire, and his face, though different in features from the first, carries the same message: *I'm one sexy mother, baby, don't you mess with me.* They don't even look dangerous. Only their weapons do. In the next picture beside them, two women: bare feet, bare legs, orange skirt, pink blouse, blue shorts, blue blouse, one fat, one thin, dumped in the road, bent ass-up over a low stone embankment, hands tied behind them, both dead. Al Haig shakes his fist. These are his enemies, and therefore yours. You study his face. He, too, killed your brother. You're not sure how. He, too, killed your paintings. You don't know, you don't remember. Your father's lost at sea. Your memory isn't right. There is a woman somewhere who imagines she loves you. But it isn't love. You don't know what it is. Obsession maybe. You think she's possessed. From the first moment he saw her he knew they would end up in bed. But it was months before he brought her up these stairs, time enough for her to cultivate a terrifying passion. In response, she claims. She scares me to death. She makes me feel like the woman. She walked to me once, through a gale. I can't shake her off. He sees her always, every time he goes out, until suddenly she's here again, inside his room, and you want your brother. My sister lives with my mother. Sole surviving son was a good deferment, a scam. She didn't need me. Doesn't. Doesn't know where I am. So what if they think I'm dead? That crate is still on her porch, decaying. They should bury it, with my brother, mark its grave with my name. His original name. If that carcass was my brother. How can I know? He's facing the wall again, staring at pictures. He rolls away, turns his back. Outside the sky's gone milky, some kind of eggshell, polar, opaque, tissue, pale, almost blue. Sky, at least. Almost the color of sky. I have a big cock. I am not dangerous. I am good in bed. You love to fuck and you run from fucking. There is never the right kind of love. There is no right kind of love. There is only the love of fucking, more fucking. There has to be something inside it, behind it. All that blood. Someday it will come down from sky. A great red cloud, like sunset, will streak across dead paper and in a sudden brief shower red rain will fall. All things that live will flourish. God will die for us again, from Heaven this time. You're crazy. Get out of bed. Eat something. Go for a walk. Find out what day it is. Go down to unemployment. What are the consequences of missing the weekly appointment? Get down there and explain. You were sick, you couldn't get up, you don't have a phone. You live way the hell and gone up here in the West End. He's sick, he can't get up, he lives alone, he has no phone. What are the consequences of going? He'll see her, on the street, it never fails. Even though she's working. She'll be on some random break. He'll go down in the morning, when the girl, at least, is in school. But Holly, he'll see her, he knows it. Holly? Is that her name? It doesn't sound right. He doesn't like it. It doesn't conjure her, but someone else, something else. An image. A paper woman. With long braids and a peasant blouse, a flowered skirt, a basket, vegetables from some pitiful garden. Some pale macrobiotic. Someone fuzzy, weak. Quiet-voiced. Small. The only thing she has in common—Holly, the real Holly—with this paper one is gold hooped earrings and glasses made with wire frames. But the real Holly's earrings are not so large, they're silver, not gold, and her glasses—what are they like now? Maybe not wire. He's seen her in plastic he thinks, dark tortoiseshell or amber. You've never seen her in wire frames. Only in old photographs. Christ, fuck it. Your memory's shot. Go downtown. Downtown. One long street. Go down into the fucking town.

He lives in a cage. Light passes through clouds in stripes. There are other women. A world of women in string bikinis with flat bellies and golden skin. Headless, fleshless, but they haunt him. One of those, he wants one of those. Or else the girl, that girl, the hard little buds inside her T-shirt, her speechless innocence, coming to knowledge. The mother's too large, too full, too loud—too much. Encompasses everything. Too like a man. Not physically, but somehow. She scares me to death. She told me about a gorilla. I live in his cage. She saw him in Buffalo. His name was Samson. If I disguised myself, combed my hair back with water, wore dark shades, a sport coat with padded shoulders, she would still know it was me, she would drop her jaw and say *Jesus Christ*. What's to expect from a woman who can tell you that once, for a while, she loved a gorilla? He sat in the corner of his cage while the cleaner approached with a hose. Cage by cage the man came, washing shit from under the primates. Samson sat in his corner, back to the oncoming man, ignoring the people, ignoring her—watching him, willing him to meet her eyes. He'd piled his shit up neatly, close to the gutter. When the man came, the gorilla scowled and the man began to curse him. In those big, gorilla eyes, she saw intelligence, suffering, shame. I fell in love with him, she said. Just for a while. Not long after, she heard he was being flown to Chicago, to live with a gorilla female. For a year, she said. They say he's depressed, she said. Mating's supposed to cure him. He's an adolescent. But what then? she wants to know. What happens to them when their year is up? When the zookeepers send Samson home? She's a remarkable person, a remarkable woman. She has a beautiful

24

daughter. I don't love her, is all. She's less than I am. Or more. She won't say she loves me, or wants love. She wants fucking, my fucking. But I don't believe her. What starts good ends badly. And she scares me. She'll swallow me up without trying. Blue, she says, get my cigarettes. If I wag my tail like a dog and I go, she'll tire of me, she'll leave. I watch her across the room. She smiles. Her green-eyed, orange-haired cat fills her lap. Her hands are stroking him and he watches me, neither of us moving. She is complete. I don't have any cigarettes, she says. She stopped smoking before I met her. I did the right thing. What if I'd stood, looked around, jumped to her whim? Would she laugh? Next time, I try it. There, she says, pointing. She started again. But it's only a dream. For a month we don't speak to each other. On the street we bat eyes, nod hello. Soon I will go to her, call her. She knows it. Because she knows it, I resist. No, I say. No. She retreats. I withhold. Nothing will happen. Nothing. Will happen. I'll go crazy if I stay in this room.

The sky is paper. The wind is up. The trees are rasping. The sand is frozen. He can't move. The wind dies and the trees get louder. He wills himself to hallucination but nothing comes. If he waits long enough something will end before he notices. Mist rises up from the ground, massive, unfolding. The light is invisible. He sees everything through panes. Beyond them, maybe nothing is flat. I think I should move. I stick one foot out from under the covers. I am cold. He retreats, curls into himself. Nothing hurts. Walls rise from the trees. Walls rise from everything visible. He bolts, leans naked against the glass. You think you are seeing the end of the world. Made of paper. You want to tear through the flatness. You slide the glass door open. The air is icy. There is no wind. In the water somewhere my father is lost. You step out onto the balcony. Cold surrounds him. If the sky opens, it will reveal more than anyone wants you to know. You think you can touch it. It is everyone's prison. He raises his hands, and you reach. The sky bleeds honey.

Earth Tides

In the beginning the sun rose over the flat earth. Adam knew it had been that way. Things changed. Not knowledge. Things themselves. Adam knew what his problem was. It was simply stated. He had lost patience with real life. He didn't know what he wanted. He sat in the desert and watched the sun and the moon. He had walked away from his work because of a single photograph. A color slide of two dead women dumped on a road. Sure, said the salesmen, working on the telephones, talking all afternoon to the papers, the news magazines. Sure, sure, we got victims, we got bodies. We got women, sure, naked legs, a fat ass and a thin one. In color? Sure, they're wearing orange and pink and blue. In the beginning, men worshiped the sun, and for a while this was good. But the presence behind the universe was jealous. The sun was Its sun, not Itself. So It changed things. Things got changed. Then knowledge. Adam had taken that photograph, had stood beside those bodies. He didn't know what he wanted, so he walked away from his work and left Karen and left New York and went up to Provincetown. The earth became a lost planet, insignificant in a universe of stars, a sudden infinity. Adam knew this. It was not man's mind that

27

changed, but its objects first. Then the mind. For a week in Provincetown he was in love with Holly but to love Holly, who had been in his thoughts for years and was his friend and was real and knew Karen, was too hard and he retreated and fucked around a while and started living with a woman he'd never known before who had great snaky eyes. And another great rift was coming. He could feel it coming. Or perhaps it had already come, was out there, waiting to be found. He still didn't know what he wanted and neither did Karen and neither did Holly and neither did the woman he was living with, and after a while he wasn't living with her anymore either, and he went back to New York to see Karen and to pack up his things, and he still didn't know what he wanted or where he was going or what he would do but he did know that when the change came everyone would know it, indistinctly, in the body, without differentiation, unable to put it into words, until some scientist, some researcher, some mathematician who was master of the necessary technical language and its tools would be able to recognize, to identify, to name this peculiar but universal change, this coming fissure, this next leaping decision on the part of the jealous presence that did not want the stars or the planets or their suns or their times or their spaces or human beings to be objects of worship. And perhaps it was not jealousy, Adam thought then, watching some desert creature that was neither plant nor animal scuttle across his field of vision, but some high sanity, requisite of order, the need of the transcendent to remain transcendent, to renew its transcendence, something like that, because if feeble man was catching up with the shape of the universe, the shape of the universe had to change. That was all. It was simple. It was obvious.

And the time had come again, because man was exhausting Its creations and confusing them with It, and Adam sometimes thought he really was in love with Holly, sometimes thought he was in love with that woman he'd lived with a while, sometimes thought the only truth was to follow everything through with Karen, and most of the time didn't think at all, going from one woman to another, except for Holly, who was seeing that guy China Blue, so finally he got on a bus and came to the southwest. He'd thought he would like the desert. He did like the desert. In the desert he gave new attention to old details: the tiny glitters of sweat in his left palm, the dry ache in his right lung, the taste of tobacco in his mouth in the morning when the only thing sweet in the room was the vodka in the coffee cup he'd taken from a diner because he didn't want to drink his vodka out of a motel room's plastic glass, when all he could see of the desert was a narrow strip of parking lot, occasional movement on the highway, a band of mauve sunrise fading to yellow and gray, when the only things moving inside were the piece of green paper fluttering on the air conditioner grill, a bead of moisture sliding down the wall of the cup into the vodka, and the nameless leftover dream creatures that looked like fragments of plant life from the scrubby Cape Cod woods but moved freely around the room like independent animals, each with a will and purpose of its own, when nothing else was moving because he would not turn on the television, because his watch had stopped days ago and he'd unplugged the clock, because he would not get up from the bed to cross the room for a cigarette now that the pack beside him was empty, to open the curtains and look for more of the desert morning, to shower or shave or wash or dress since there was nowhere he wanted to go, nowhere he had to go, nowhere he would go at all now until the vodka was gone because although he knew it was an alcoholic stunt to trip three thousand miles across the country just to hole up in some motel room drinking, he drank his vodka slowly and didn't care. There were other things to contemplate, more pressing than the poisons in his body, and he had no obligations, and the poisons weren't his master. He knew he had a long life to live yet. So much was undone, undreamed of. The vodka didn't matter. It was just there, like cigarettes, like the ache in his lung, the sweat in his palm, like the cars passing on the highway more frequently now and the mauve band of light rising on another artificial day, but here in the desert, in his room, he saw a different day, a day more real, wet, a winter day when the boats go out, when the tide is low and coming in, when the water is slate and silver, when the seagull's cry is the only thing eternal and the bare branches of garden plants and bushes and trees and wild things tremble in a breath of air too withdrawn and self-contained to be a wind. The air is cold on this day he sees and the cats in the morning are prowling the beaches and streets and yards, black cats, orange cats, gray cats, and all the black and white ones. There are not so many dogs, but on the sidewalks, brick-colored clumps of dog shit. There is something to this winter stillness. Something is, and he is listening for it, until the desert day rises so high in him he has to move, sits, refills his cup, crosses the room for a fresh pack of cigarettes, drops it to the dresser again as soon as he's picked it up, scratches his head, goes to the toilet and pisses, splashes cold water on his face, dries his face looking in the mirror, sees that tears stain his shirt and knows last night he must have cried, looks at the face in the mirror and knows it is not his face but the face of some witness to his life, some sullen comrade who can never cooperate but won't go away, who like the surface of the earth moves with the moon, who watches him with suspicion, withholding something Adam would very much like him to say, until he leaves the mirror, the bathroom, picks up the cigarette pack, the book he's been reading, and carries them to bed. I'm not afraid of anything, Holly said in bed, rising over him, surrounding him, I *am* in love with you. But Nijinsky writes *I am not afraid of anything, and want to die.* Nijinsky knows himself as one of the clowns of God, who express love and not hate. *A clown without love is not from God*, Nijinsky writes. *I will be ready for everything*, he writes. *God wishes to improve life and I will be his instrument.* Nijinsky was crazy. *I know that everyone will be frightened of me and they will put me into a lunatic asylum*, Nijinsky writes, *but I do not care.* Nijinsky was lucid. *My soul is ill*, he writes. *My soul, not my mind.* I'm not afraid of anything, I *am* in love with you, Holly said when he asked was she afraid he would fall in love with her because she had just told him she was feeling strange and shy. They were naked. They were tumbling into bed. He was lying on his back and she took him into herself and they were still and All of a sudden I feel shy with you, she said. Maybe you're afraid I'll fall in love with you? he said. And suddenly she was all joy—I'm not afraid of anything, I am in love with you, and I have been for a real long time—and he knew mid-sentence where her sentence would end and he spoke the last words with her, *for a real long time.* But Nijinsky is not afraid of anything and wants to die. Nijinsky is crazy from the beginning, from his opening words: *People will say that Nijinsky pretends to be mad on account of his bad deeds. Bad deeds are terrible and I hate them, and do not want to commit any.* Simplicity is always mad. Nijinsky is a child. He contradicts himself from sentence to sentence. In his great confusion, he confuses himself with God. He is not mad. He is not a child. He is simple and lucid. God's clown. A holy fool. Not to be afraid of anything is to be a holy fool. To be in love is to be a holy fool. To want to die is to be a holy fool. That is no despairing desire in the madman's sentence. It is a wanting to die that is holy, that is foolish, that is all love. Holiness is error, folly is error, love is error. They let you live like that a while and then they drive you back into your cage. Adam is thirty-four years old, five years older than Nijinsky, and still alive, functioning, surviving, still surviving. He's even kept his VISA card. Nijinsky should have had a VISA card. It would have gotten him by for a while, as it gets Adam by now. Sooner or later he'll have to call New York, tell Florida where he is, get some money. Sooner or later he'll have to find a job, a woman, anything. When the time comes, it will be urgent and real, insistent, demanding that he buck up, survive, but for now what's real is not this late fall day in the desert but a deep winter day in the east when the world as everyone knows it might end; not the skittering dream creatures conjured by this parallel but different world of rock and sand, but the cry of seagulls and a breathless wind; not the solitude here, but the women back there, as if only here, in this solitude, can those women become real; not the heat of this desert sun, but the ice, the acid in that air and ground, and the sudden heat that's manmade and primed to burn. It's the future he's listening for but he can't listen far enough. He's training himself to know that real life doesn't exist. *Existence itself mocks ev-*

eryone who is engaged in becoming purely objective. Kierkegaard wrote that sentence a hundred and one years before Adam was born. Now the whole world was engaged in becoming purely objective and existence was howling, preparing its next big cosmic joke. It was time for the change. Perhaps, yes, it had already taken place. Sitting out there in the desert he'd begun to feel it, to know it, but to know the taste of it, the feel of it, was not to describe it, to give it a name, and so he'd gone back, but back to nothing. Karen was seeing some new guy and didn't know what she wanted—five years and she didn't know what she wanted, all that love and all that grief and she didn't know what she wanted; the snake-eyed woman he'd lived with a while didn't want him coming around now, any more than he wanted going; and Holly was still seeing that strange China Blue. It was time for the change. Maybe, yes, it had already taken place. Maybe, yes, everybody knew. But no one had the language, the science, the precision to define it, to know this thing that everybody knew, and no one would have until the rupture went public, found its revealer, making new revolutions—social, political, theological—as always before, so Adam got on another bus and rode it back west where doing nothing now he waits for reality to heave itself up and shed skin, explode, shatter, bang itself to smithereens and bloom.

December Woman

I met him in a bar, where I've met every lover I've had since I came to this town. I figured it would end in a bar, too. Things have a way of doing that. He wasn't exactly handsome, just inevitable. There was something uncanny, a stillness, about him. I saw secrets in his eyes. Face it, I wanted him. Anyone would. But his body didn't have a lot to do with it. I'm not even sure I'd say he was much of a lover. Not objectively. But, Jesus. I've never had a lover like him.

It was a Thursday afternoon, the end of April, the day after Megan Riley got stabbed. I was sitting in the Bradford, at the bar, and that stabbing was all anyone could talk about. He was sitting there too. Alone. Maybe not even listening. Just drinking his drink. I got to watching him, that was all. I was with a bunch of bozos, listening to the talk. Some of us had seen Lonnie Johnson in there the night before. We all knew Lonnie a little. He'd been around here twenty years. We knew the woman. Not well, I mean, but the way you do around this town. We knew they'd been going together, lived together. We knew she had kids, teenagers, boys. So I was listening for a change. The bozos had more to talk about than usual. But I was also thinking about my own self and about those boys of hers and thinking about Jesse and wondering if he'd ever get a

35

chance to grow up even that old, seventeen, nineteen—man aged.

I was missing Jesse pretty bad then. They took him away in winter when I freaked, and I didn't know if I'd ever get him back. They locked me up to dry out and when they let me go I was on GA instead of AFDC and they'd taken Jesse and put him in a foster home. They said it was temporary. I was supposed to go to AA and stop hanging out in bars. I said they had no right and didn't listen to what they told me. It was Adam that found out what I had to do. I mean, he wanted to help me get my kid back. But that all comes later. That day after Megan Riley died he was just a stranger I was watching while I listened to the talk. He was listening too, I thought, and it looked like it was really getting to him—this guy who sees red because his girlfriend leaves him, who goes to see her where he thinks she's with another man, who's carrying a knife and knifes her, who she runs from, who chases her out to the sidewalk and knifes her some more. Twenty-six stab wounds. In her head, face, chest, back, belly. In five minutes, maybe. She was dead. The thing was, Lonnie was a nice guy, he'd been around for years, he drank with cops, he called Chief Deeds Billy to his face. I mean, he was liked, you know, not getting in trouble, not some wharf rat roaming the streets and getting in fights and breaking windows all winter long. He was a cook in one of the best summer restaurants. Responsible. Serious. So everyone was shocked. You could almost tell from the faces on the street that day who knew him and Megan together and how well. In the bar, they're the ones who don't have much to say.

Me, I'm just sitting there listening and thinking about Jesse and watching this guy drink his drink and I get to thinking he's a good-looking guy, kind of scruffy, all rumpled, with brownish

36

hair, and I've seen him before probably and never noticed. I'm thinking about saying something to him, not really thinking what, just thinking of getting up and going over to the empty barstool beside him and sitting down, saying anything. And then he glances up. As if he's felt me watching. He just looks at me and catches me looking. Normally you'd look away or move your eyes slow, cruising the room, or smile suddenly or shrug or wink, raise your glass, ask for a light, anything, but the funny thing is I just kept looking—as if we'd been looking at each other for hours, I just kept on looking back. He was smoking a cigarette. His look was blank, not leering or that I'm-going-to-pick-you-up-tonight stare, or like you're a piece of meat either or some kind of freak, none of that, just plain, blank looking. Then he finished his cigarette and stood up. He reached in his pocket and put some coins on the bar. He picked up his pack of Winstons. He put his fatigue jacket on and walked out. He didn't look back. He didn't look at me from the moment he stood up. But I was watching for him after that. I even had a dream about him, and the next time I saw him there, maybe after two days, maybe the next week, I went over and said hello. He said hello back, as if he knew me, and we sat together at the bar for five hours, talking and drinking vodka till we were the last people in there and I asked if he didn't want to come up to my place and drink and talk some more. He blinked, as if he was surprised, and said yes, yes he did. He slept with me that night without even really touching me but in the morning when we got up he grabbed my wrist and asked was he supposed to take off his clothes. I laughed then and I guess he thought it was funny too. He grinned, like Jesse used to when he knew he'd done something he could get away with if he was cute enough, ducking his head down and not looking me in the eyes.

When Adam did look at me though, the grin was gone and he sounded sorry: I'm kind of screwed up about love right now, he said.

Love? I said.

Yeah, he said. What about love?

Love, I said. Love's never been anything but trouble.

That's how it started. We got up and we still hadn't touched each other except curled up sleeping and his hand around my wrist. Maybe he did love me. Maybe he didn't. I don't think it matters. I don't think he even knew and I don't think that matters either.

You have a kid? he said. He nodded toward Jesse's crayon drawings taped to the refrigerator.

He isn't with me now, I said, and that was all. I poured him a cup of coffee.

It was a bright, clear morning. Hard sunlight slanted through the curtains making long, patterned shadows on the floor. The crystal hanging in the window shot colors into his face where he sat smoking at the table. He kept looking at me, sitting there drinking his coffee while I cooked, and neither of us said anything until I put his plate down in front of him.

Don't you want to talk about it? he said and I said No, I guess I don't.

The night before in the crowd at the bar we'd talked for hours—about L.A., and Elvis Presley, Bobby Kennedy, something about Europe I guess, and New York, which was where he'd just come from, I don't know what all, odds and ends, and now here we were, sitting in my kitchen with the steaming potatoes and eggs and coffee and cigarettes and peace and quiet and we didn't have a single thing to say. He wanted to know about Jesse, I guess. He just watched me moving around, watched me eat. Then all of a sudden he said Tell me something that happened to you when you were six.

Six? I said—nothing happened to me when I was six, I was thinking—and he kept looking at me, and then there it was, that look, and I knew he had me. He knew it too. We went back to bed.

After that, it just was. He wasn't really living anywhere, just staying with friends, anywhere they had room. There was a woman in New York he was trying to leave. He'd lived with her for years, until he started thinking he had to be alone. Whatever he did was for that—he just didn't know how to bring it off.

I laughed when he told me. You want to leave, I said, leave. It's easy. Men do it all the time.

He shook his head. It's not like that, he said.

It? I said. What? You? Her? The world? The world's like that— believe it.

Tell me about your son, he said.

Let's go get a drink, I said.

Don't fight me, he said.

I looked at him again. It was morning again. The window was open. It was May by then. A warm breeze was billowing the curtains. Rainbows from the crystal moved across his cheek.

It's too early to get a drink, he said.

Like hell, I said.

He sighed. I've never known a man to sigh like that. Like a slow wind dying, like a woman after labor, like the end of the world.

What do you want from me? I said.

He smiled and his eyes came back to life. He reached for his jacket where it hung behind him on the chair.

Where're you going? I said.

What's it to you? he said and he was already standing and bending down to kiss my cheek.

Don't get soft with me, I said.

I'll be back, he said, and he was, three days later, stoned, tired, drunk and carrying a full bottle, one almost empty, three joints, an *Advocate* and a bag of tomatoes.

Took me a while, he said. Tomorrow, tell me about your son.

Where'd you get this stuff? I asked when I walked into the kitchen in the morning and found him sitting at the table, smoking a joint, everything still spread out the way he'd dumped it when he came in the night before. In New York he'd worked at a photo agency. He still had some money, I guess, but not much. Mostly those few days we'd been together he lived on me.

Did a little work, he said. Helped a man paint a deck.

He emptied his pockets onto the table, four crumpled bills and lots of loose change. All I have is yours, he said. Then he smiled and said he was sorry, he'd meant to come back sooner.

I sat down and looked at him over the vodka bottles. There was no way to be mad at him, nothing to be mad at him for. He reminded me of Jesse. There was something so clear in his way with me, as if he knew me inside out. Or didn't have to know me. Just took me as I seemed. One hundred percent. The way a child takes his mother, before he's old enough to wish she was somebody else.

I started fingering the money, smoothing out the bills. Two of them were twenties.

How do you pay the rent? he said.

He knew we were eating off food stamps. He knew I got GA. He knew it wasn't much. I said it used to help to screw the landlord. He didn't laugh. The rent's still pretty low, I said. In summer when I could, I've turned a few tricks, but I didn't tell him that.

Do you work in summer? he asked.

I'm not good for much, I said.

Neither am I, he said. He smiled then, full of light, and looked at me a while.

Can I stay here then? he asked.

I laughed. You are staying here, aren't you?

He shrugged and didn't answer. He picked up the roach and lit it and passed it, watching my eyes.

I need a place to be for a while, he said.

You're here, I said.

He nodded. I couldn't tell what he was asking for.

I'm trying to leave this woman in New York, he said.

You told me, I said.

Tell me about your son, he said.

I can't, I said. He's not here. I can't get him back.

How do you know? he said.

I don't want to argue, I said.

How do you feel about it?

Leave me alone, I said.

I could see it made him sad that I wouldn't talk about it. But I couldn't. I wanted him to understand.

Like you don't want to talk about that woman in New York, I said.

But one way or another, the question always came back. Maybe

I'd be telling him some story and I'd mention Jesse. Then Adam would say What *about* Jesse? Or he'd be talking about this woman he might have loved who had a teenage daughter and he'd make some remark about never having had kids himself and then he'd say it must have been hard, losing my son. I couldn't even get mad at him for it, and finally anyhow I told him about the freakout in winter and getting sent to Bridgewater. He wanted to know about Bridgewater but I hardly remembered.

They had me on some drug, I said.

I kept having these crazy ideas. I thought everything meant something, every little thing. I thought whatever I saw or heard was an order sent to me straight from the Devil or from God. When they let me out of there, I got better. I started drinking again as soon as I hit the street.

But I told him all that later. Deep in summer. That morning in May all I did was refuse to discuss it and get up for glasses and ice.

She's in El Salvador, he said behind me.

Thanks, I said.

She photographs wars, he said.

I turned and looked at him. He shrugged. He said, I'll tell you anything you want.

I said, Tell me what she's doing with a bum like you, and he laughed.

They get shellshocked, he said. Ordinary people don't make sense anymore.

I went back to the table and emptied the opened bottle and handed him a drink.

She thinks I'm just up here for a while, he said. She thinks I'm coming home.

And what about you? I said. What do you think?

I don't know, he said. He smiled at me. The sunlight traced a bright line around his curly, fuzzy hair. I don't know what I think, he said, I don't know what I'm doing, I don't know anything at all.

He sounded very simple saying that—cheerful, matter-of-fact. The way he said that made me laugh. But then he said Tell me what you've ever done that's made you feel ashamed.

Ashamed? I said. I wanted to keep on laughing. Well, I said, there was the time I got laid by this bartender I hardly knew at three in the morning on top of a pool table. It was sort of a carom effect, I said, trying to be funny. But Adam wanted to know what I really meant.

I got some great news that day, I told him.

I didn't really want to talk about it, about any of it, but Adam had a way of getting me going.

I got some great news, I said, so I went to the bar looking for someone to tell it to, looking for Jerry really, this guy I was half in love with, and when I got there he was in the driveway in his pickup getting ready to head out of town. Come water the garden with me, he said. This was in Ohio, eight, nine years ago. So tell me what's so great, he said when I climbed in, but when I told him he just laughed and in the garden all he wanted was to eat me there in the sunset with the baby tomatoes and corn.

He was a good man, Jerry, but that evening I got pissed and walked away, back the mile or so to the bar, where I ran into another guy, a college kid I knew who was trying to be an artist and who said That's great when I told him my news. He really did seem to understand why I was excited, and we got to talking until he said why didn't I come down to his studio and see his work? And that's where we were, sort of fooling around, when his girlfriend I didn't even know existed showed up all flare-eyed and the guy said Later, shooing me out the door. He'll see me in the bar downstairs maybe, he whispers, if I want to wait around, so that's where I'm sitting, alone in this bar with the pool table where I end up getting laid.

So boom boom boom, I said to Adam. Jerry's the one I want and I end up with a stranger, the bartender, this blond guy with leering eyes.

So tell me about Jerry, Adam said.

Jerry? I said. I didn't really want to talk about him, but Adam always won.

He was a vet, I said. Vietnam. That always got to me back then. Before the war he'd meant to be a photographer, and his friends from back then said he was good. But by the time I knew him all he cared about was that garden, drinking, and getting laid. He never would talk about the war and he never took another picture. Not even for fun.

I looked at Adam across the table. You remind me of him a little, I said, but Adam said Shellshock? sounding so sarcastic I just went What?

Shellshock never makes them quit, he said. They go out looking for more.

I was about to ask if he'd been in the war. He was the right age. Maybe he saw the question coming. He didn't answer it. Instead he said So why did Jerry quit? and I said Why did you?

Me? he said. I never was a photographer.

Your job, I said. Why did you quit your job.

Oh, that, he said.

44

You get used to anything, he said. And then one day you snap. He walked away from his job because of a photograph. A color slide of two dead women dumped on a road. He stopped being used to it. He didn't know what he wanted. He stood up from his desk and took his jacket off the back of his chair and walked. On the street he didn't know where he was. He didn't pay attention. That night he called Karen in her hotel room in San Salvador. The next morning he rented out their apartment and at one o'clock he got on the bus.

So that's why I quit, he said. For no good reason. That's my story, he said. Go on with yours.

I shrugged. I said What's left? It's one a.m., everyone else is clearing out, the student guy is a no-show and before I know what's happening I'm getting screwed with my ass down naked on that felt.

Then Adam asked what my good news had been and I laughed and said I didn't suppose it mattered now, maybe it never did.

He looked at me like he didn't believe me. I saw how pale his eyes were. I melted a little. I said maybe sometime later I'd tell him, and he shook his head at me and sighed. Then we went to bed and had our best fuck yet. He was careful, real slow, real close to me and real turned on. I guess that pool table did it to him, I don't know.

Later, when we got up and washed and went out we headed up toward Spiritus for pizza. It was a hot, bright day. The street was crowded and everyone looked happy—happier than late in summer when every place is packed with people trying too hard to have a good time and everyone else is working too hard and dying for winter. Adam saw the same thing and he was happy too because he'd just put his hand on my shoulder and his mouth to my ear when a woman roller skated into us and between us, her hands holding her belly, covered with blood.

We turned, watching her break through the crowd, Adam going as white as if it was him that was bleeding. She left blood all over the street. After a minute, without saying anything, we followed her, back the way we'd come. She'd skated to the police station, downstairs in Town Hall. We knew it as soon as the siren sounded. Adam's color came back. As if that siren meant some kind of safety.

In the Bradford I ordered a beer, but Adam didn't want anything. His hands were shaking and he took his pack of cigarettes out of his shirt pocket and fumbled in his pants. The bartender asked What happened out there? and tossed him a book of matches, but Adam just caught them and walked away.

It was a weird violent spring. A few weeks later, a guy blew his head off with a .38 revolver and the first day of June a fifty-year-old man who lived with his mother was arrested for stabbing her to death with a rigging knife.

Each time we heard about one of these incidents, Adam got real quiet. Then he'd go out and do some kind of work, painting, that kind of thing, and come home each night feeling better. He didn't drink so much with me then, when he was working, and sometimes he'd sit at the table watching me with a look on his face like he didn't know who I was or what I was doing in this room in his life. Then he'd ask me some question, like that Tell me something that happened when you were six, and get me talking, and after a while he'd be talking too and we'd start drinking vodka together and laughing and by the time the painting job ended we'd be having a pretty good time again. I did a little cleaning then, too, for my landlord, who's got a lot of summer places and even though I'm not the greatest likes to give me work because he knows it means he'll see his rent. Most of the kind of tenants he gets don't care much anyway, so everybody's happy, and between odds and ends like that and my GA and food stamps, Adam and I made it through the summer eating pretty well and smoking and drinking as much as we wanted. The only thing that bothered me—and it was funny because it never happened before—was when I went to clean the bathrooms and found a shower curtain drawn, I had to hold my breath and tighten my stomach for fear when I pulled it open I'd find some chopped-up body swimming in blood.

When I told Adam that, he got real tender and said it didn't sound like me, and then he asked what in my life had ever made me afraid.

Maybe it was that clear calm look on his face, the innocence, I don't know, but answering him I went way back, to the end of the sixties and people I hadn't thought about in years.

I was living in this communal apartment building in Berkeley and one night we all did some blue powdered mescaline an old boyfriend had given me folded up loose in a sheet of paper. I was going to school then, and so were some of the others, but life in that family always seemed more real than anything ever had been, and school didn't really exist. Most of the others that night were going over to San Francisco to hear Janis Joplin and they just did a little in capsules but Johnny and I—we were lovers and kind of crazy then—we stayed home and ate that powder in big fingerfuls until it was gone.

I laughed telling Adam.

That powder, I said, was the color of your eyes.

Then Johnny and I went to see his friends in the house down the block, and he disappears into the kitchen, leaving me to space out where I am—

47

sprawled in an armchair under a green light, listening to some woman blues singer and staring at my arm hanging motionless off the chair. After a while, I forget I'm not alone. When I suddenly remember that one of the women from the house is sitting stiff and silent in the corner on the floor, I get the creeps. I want Johnny to come back. I want to go to him. I'm looking at my hand, my arm frozen, green. I think: I can't move. I think: My body is a corpse. I think: If I don't move right now I'll sit in this chair all night and in the morning everyone will find me in it dead. I want to say something to the woman but I know she won't hear me, only Johnny will hear me because only Johnny ate that powder, because only Johnny is with me, only Johnny can understand. I know my body's trapped, and in the morning I'll be dead. I'm calm. Then suddenly I bolt for the kitchen. Pushing through the swinging door, I see the look on Johnny's face. I can't open my mouth. I can't say a word. I can only see his terror and turn and run.

My feet never touched the sidewalk. I'd left my body in that chair. That house was full of witches. They made me fly. I was moving faster than I ever had in my life but I had to run forever to get home.

Upstairs I found Maggie and Jenny and tried to say what was wrong. But I was moving too fast for them. All they heard was babble. It can't be mescaline, one of them says, it must be speed, and to me they say Calm down, it's only a bad drug, and You just ate too much of it, it'll burn off, and nothing they say has anything to do with what's happening to me.

I stop listening. I'm alone. I already died. My body's down the street turning green.

It makes me laugh now, I said to Adam that Sunday in the heat.

I gave up. I let them put me on the floor, let them play a record and put the headphones on my ears. They go downstairs and leave me. I'm lying on my back. My eyes are closed. I'm looking at nothing, big and black, when angels start appearing, golden faces circling the void. It's the angels who are singing. A song to my dying, welcoming me to death. I'm happy. The angels want me. They want my body to let me go. I love the way they call to me. My body begins to open. I begin to rise away from it. I'm in ecstasy. Except my heart is pounding too hard, too fast. I can hear my blood and a crackling in the music in my ears. My body is resisting. The static is resisting. My heart is beating so fast because for me to go to the angels my body has to die. I want to go to the angels, I want to give myself up to them. It's not the angels who scare me, but my body moving so fast it's going to explode. Then out of nowhere I hear myself screaming for help. Help! I'm screaming, not from my head, not me, but my body, without thought, without intention, from deep in my belly, loud and hollow—Help! over and over, until Jenny's there beside me pulling the headphones off my ears, and sitting cross-legged, holding me in her arms and lap, she rocks me back and forth like a baby.

I got very calm after that. I lay down on the couch under some blankets and got to wondering what it would have been like to have had a mother like that, a mother who would hold you in her arms and let you weep and shake and cry. Because all my life, I loved my old man. My mother was cold, very distant and high class. We lived in Pasadena. The living room was white, even the furniture. The rug was white and two inches thick. No lie. Purple was the only color in there, purple throw pillows, purple flowers, purple glass. Even the cat was white. You couldn't say boo in that room. And my mother loved that cat better than she ever loved me. I didn't fit the decor. I wasn't part of her wardrobe or one of her props. I was big and ungainly and rowdy and loud. She had silver hair from before I was born. She was tan and thin and beautiful. The perfect ice mother. These same high cheekbones. I always think of her like that room, white and purple, even though she wore every color under the sun—

Suddenly I stopped talking. I lit a cigarette and fanned my damp T-shirt away from my skin.

Go on, Adam said softly. Tears were forming in his eyes. Tell me more.

How do you know there is more? I said.

He didn't answer. The tears spilled down his cheeks and he didn't lift a hand to wipe them away. They were silent tears, the kind that come without wanting them, the kind most people never let you see.

I couldn't get used to being with a man who cared so much.

After a while, I told him, I got up and phoned the guy who gave me the powder. I was still babbling, but he said Take a cab on me. When I got there he wanted to give me thorazine, but I said Are you crazy? Some chemical did this to me, you think I want more? so he took me to bed and we fucked and I got better, and all the while we were fucking I kept seeing Johnny's face.

I never did understand where that scream came from. Once it started, I said to Adam, it wouldn't stop. I few mornings later, on the way to German lit, I turned around and went to the psych center and never went to another class. Four times I saw this old lady of a shrink and the only thing I remember about those sessions is when she looked me in the eye and said Why are you so hostile? as if being hostile was a crime. I didn't know I was hostile until she said that but I answered Why shouldn't I be? and got up and walked out.

Why are you so hostile? Adam asked, but all I did was laugh.

It was something, the way he could get me talking, remembering. Once when I was holding back a story he said You should never be ashamed of anyone you've made love to. He was that innocent. But sometimes you have to be.

What about Johnny? he asked when I finished that story.

Johnny? I said. That night he had the shakes, I guess, and after a while he sort of disappeared. A long time later, my first winter here, I sometimes thought I saw him on the street. Then I heard he got shot, back in Berkeley. Some drug thing, maybe. I don't know.

It's years since I've even thought about all this, I said, those angels, Johnny, my mother, that shrink. My mother died from drugs herself, I said, a few years later, barbiturates and alcohol, and then before long my father married someone else, someone more like him, and more like me.

Don't get me wrong, I said. I'm not much like him now, or her either, but then I thought I still had some kind of chance. It gave me the idea I could do something to save my life, his marrying that woman who was all I could and should have been but wasn't.

That's when I realized Adam never forgot a thing. Out of nowhere he said So what was your great news?

It seemed so foolish and trivial, I didn't want to tell him. I shrugged and stood up to get a drink.

Don't, he said. Come on.

Nothing, I said. I shrugged again. I couldn't look at him. The air was heavy, muggy and hot. From the street we heard voices, a horn honking, music from the nearest bar. The windows were open and we hadn't turned the lights on. The room was dusky and blue and still a little orange from the last of the sunset. Inside we were silent. Finally I said I just thought I was going back to school.

School, he said. He fingered the handle of the mug he'd been drinking cold coffee out of. Did you like school? he said.

Yeah, I said, in a funny way I did. I looked him in the face then. I smiled. I was pretty smart in those days, I said.

You're still pretty smart, he said, and we laughed.

But you didn't go? he said.

I went to Europe that summer, I said. As if that was the answer. And maybe it was.

I was looking at his hands, at his nails, broad and flat, at the square tips of his fingers, at his skin, freckled and so pale in the shadows it was blue. They were hands that would never hurt me.

Let's lie down, I said, and Adam said You sound like a little girl.

The room was dark. The only light was coming from the street. I almost cried. Don't ask me why.

Tell me about Europe, he said.

Later, I said. Tomorrow.

My daddy wanted to stake me to the trip. He was that glad I was going back to school. I'd put it all together on my own, without asking his advice, without telling him I was doing it until after it was done. When I said I'd get financial aid, he told me not to worry, he'd help with anything I needed, and then he offered me this trip. I lied and said I had some money saved and only took half what he wanted to give me.

Maybe I was just too old for traveling poor. Or I'd seen too much street life already in San Francisco. Lying around the park in Amsterdam smoking dope with hundreds of other American hippie types just didn't turn me on. So I'd get taken home by some guy instead.

There were good things for a while, I said to Adam. Art and museums, random conversations, trying to use languages, ideas that would hit me as if they were brand new. At first I really did think I was going back. I took books with me, to get psyched for school. I read them, too, in parks and cafes, on ferries—Sartre, Beckett, Kierkegaard—stuff like that. I carried a camera. I took pictures, black and whites. I was going to learn to use a darkroom when I got back to Berkeley. But it was all a game. I even kept a notebook for a while, till I lost it in Cologne.

Outside it was raining, a hard, late-summer rain. We had a full bottle of vodka and nowhere to go. I went on talking.

The trouble started before I ever left the country, when I was hanging out in New York waiting for my plane. I went to an opening for some lousy art and drank a bunch of wine and went home with the gallery director to an uptown apartment plastered with photographs of him with his girlfriend and her two little girls. He told me they were out of town, it was their apartment, and I walked away in the morning wishing I'd dosed him with some disease. On the ferry from Ostende to Dover, a fellow gave me the eye and when I smiled back, he said he was the second mate, he had a cabin and a bottle of gin, why not enjoy the crossing down below? I never refused an invitation. An Irish guy up against a haystack, a Jamaican on a London rooftop, two Iranian carpet merchants who when I was leaving wanted to pay me like a whore. They were brothers. Hassan and Hussein. I met them on a street in London one sunny afternoon. They took turns with me. I counted. I got fucked eleven times. Maybe that's when it hit me, I don't know, but by the time the summer ended I wasn't good for anything but sex and drinking. I drifted everywhere, all the way to Algeria, and I didn't go home and I got to knowing I wasn't free—I'd never been free, my life had never had anything to do with freedom, all those words I thought I was living were empty, fake, not about me, about someone else maybe, something else. Persian, one of those Iranians said I was, and he meant something good by it, something lavish and generous and full of warmth and spirit, but to me it just meant I was a whore.

I want to hear about them, Adam said.

I didn't want to tell this story. Somehow Adam got it out of me that day while it rained. He got every story out of me and not one of them seemed to matter.

I was walking around with my camera, I said. I was in Picadilly, I think, when this dark good-looking man came up to me saying *Sprechen Sie Deutsch?* I answered, slow and groping, *Ein Bisschen, ich bin eine Amerikanerin*, and he called out Hussein! and waved to a wild-looking curly-haired guy who was leaning up against the wall of a pub. Hussein ran over grinning and explained in English: the good-looking one was his brother, he had just arrived in London the week before. He was lonely here. He could speak only German and Italian. Would I have a drink with them, and keep Hassan a little company?

I looked at Hassan—a beautiful man, more attractive than his wild-haired English-speaking brother. He smiled at me, almost shy. He asked me please in German, said it would make him very happy. I said my German wasn't very good, but I didn't hesitate for long.

It turned out Hassan had lived six months in Munich, and before that six in Milan. They had plenty of money. They traded in Persian rugs. Hussein spent his time in London when he wasn't in Tehran. On the second round of drinks, he said he had to go to Heathrow, would I take care of Hassan for a while? We could all have dinner together, he said, and I said I'd cook it and took Hassan shopping in Portobello Road. We wandered through the open stalls, talking to each other in broken German, me translating when we talked with the vendors, and I loved the great bright beautiful exotic domesticity of it, to be so far from home, so separated from everyone who knew me, walking around with this handsome stranger, talking together in a language that was neither of our own, checking out vegetables and asking prices, Hassan paying, carrying the bags, and everyone treating us like people who belonged together, like people who shared some kind of life.

Then we left the market and Hassan hailed a cab and started pawing me as soon as we got in it. I didn't care. They're really roomy, English cabs. I liked him. He turned me on. We were going to Hampstead, to the flat his brother shared with their British partner. I must have been wearing a dress that day, because by the time we got there Hassan had my panties down around my ankles and his fingers up my crotch. I stuffed the panties into a grocery bag while he paid the driver, followed him to the door, and inside got laid on the orange living-room rug.

The place felt like my mother's house: a big fancy split-level job, very clean and high-tech, impersonal and cold. While Hassan disappeared to shower and change his clothes, I concocted myself a drink of Tanqueray and Cointreau and started the lamb chops soaking in garlic and lemon. I made a salad. I had the artichokes washed and ready to steam when Hussein got home. The three of us sat around drinking, carrying on a wild trilingual conversation, nothing fully translated, everything going two ways at once. Maybe while we ate, I began to understand. I don't know exactly when it was, what was said, what gesture made. Maybe it was Hassan himself. Maybe I followed him into the bedroom and got told to entertain his brother first. Or maybe it was later, after we'd made love again, when Hussein came naked into the bedroom to show me how hard and big he was, begging me to let him in. No, I said, no, but while Hassan and I lay there looking through his snapshots—the red racing car he drove in Munich, the girlfriend in Milan he said he loved—I could hear Hussein in his room upstairs weeping. I lay still and listened until Hassan started kissing my neck and ears and whispering in German Go to him. Go. I still didn't want to, not the way he meant, and he got hard again anyway and kept me a while longer, but when we were done I got to thinking about those precious images he'd been showing me and how they looked just as slick and safe as he did, got to thinking he was just a shallow pretty guy, all surface, no inside, while upstairs this crazy passionate Hussein was alone, crying and crying.

Maybe it was an act, I don't know, but it started to work on me. I went up. I just meant to talk to him, to try to calm him down, to say it wasn't anything, it wasn't important, but he got to me, crying like that. It *wasn't* nothing, not to him, and suddenly, even though I didn't really want him, I asked myself why not? and crawled in between his sheets.

When I came down, I found Hassan watching television, some horror flick with Christopher Lee. Chris Topher Lee, he kept saying, going on about how much he liked him, and still watching the movie he screwed me on the beanbag chair and sent me back to his brother. They traded me off all night long, and in the morning they wanted to give me money.

No, I kept saying. No, no, no, and Hussein called me Persian and wouldn't let me leave. He made me take a shirt, a bracelet, and five pounds for a cab I knew I wouldn't spend it on. I promised to send them blue jeans from America. Real Levis, they wanted. They gave me their phone number. They wanted me to call. They were good, I mean. It wasn't their fault.

And what's funny is, I said to Adam, after all my indifference and resistance, Hussein's the one I most remember, he's the one I think was real.

Damaged goods, you'd think he'd say. Other men have said it. But Adam was different. He'd been around the barn a few too many times himself. He'd blown every good thing he ever had by accepting all the stray invitations that came along. Just like me. Maybe that was it, I don't know. But he listened and he didn't judge. Not about that anyway. He really didn't care. We sat in my kitchen drinking vodka and smoking and when we ran out we'd go down to the bar and drink and smoke some more. We drank slow and talked and listened and finally we'd go to bed. We didn't always make love. Sometimes he never even took off his clothes. He had things on his mind. He talked some, too, but mostly he asked questions. Whatever was bugging him, he kept it to himself. Maybe it was the future, I don't know. He never talked about the future, or even much about the present. Just old things. Old love affairs, childhood, things like that. And he listened to my life. As if he had to absorb it all, my life in words, listen, listen, listen till I couldn't think of another thing to say. For a while I told him my dreams. Then they dried up too. As if they couldn't even be dreamed anymore, knowing they'd end up told to him.

I don't think he meant for it to happen. It was just the difference between us we couldn't understand. I didn't know what it would be, only that it had to come. Maybe I did know. Because it was the thing I saved for last.

Of course, whenever that came, it would have been the last. But by the time I got to it, nothing else was left. I lost my father over Jesse, and in the end I lost Adam over Jesse too.

I remember the night I first opened up about him. Underneath, it was the same old question: Where had Jesse come from, why was he gone, where was he now?

I came home from Europe down to nothing but my return trip ticket and worn out from scrounging. I went back to that small Ohio town. I wrote tearful letters to Daddy, full of remorse for blowing his confidence, letters I recognized as less than half true. And he forgave me. He even came to visit that spring, after a business trip to Chicago. It's the last I saw of him. I didn't know how hard I'd grown until that morning he arrived. He'd rented a car at the airport and driven to town, and the first thing he did when he got there was take me for a ride. He didn't say much. I think he liked driving because he had to watch the road.

What are you planning to do? he asked, and when I was done telling him, he dropped me off at my apartment and drove back to Dayton and flew away.

What was I planning to do? Adam wanted to know, and there we were.

Jesse, I said.

It was that simple. I was pregnant. The father could have been any one of four men, none of whom I wanted in my life. An old friend from Berkeley was living here, so here is where I came. I did it on purpose. I went on welfare, had that baby, and stayed and stayed.

My father wanted me to have an abortion.

For what? I said to him.

Maybe Jesse was just my meal ticket, I said to Adam, and even though the room was only lit by a candle I could see the tears welling up behind his eyes. I wanted to laugh. I was coming into a fury and I could feel it rising. But then we heard the sirens and got up off the bed and went into the kitchen and found it getting strobed by red and orange light.

The summer was full of fires. The one across the street wasn't the first or the last. Maybe it was the biggest, I don't know, it was the only one I saw. It started in a restaurant, no one knew how, and then it spread. It was late, after hours. No one was in there, but two guys who lived upstairs had to be carried out by firemen. We watched it from the windows a while, then put our clothes on and went down into the street, Adam close beside me, his arm around my waist, his face burnt gold by the flames and flashing lights.

The night got eerie as the fire settled, the street deserted except for the firemen and people who'd come out from their beds like Adam and me, the rescue vehicles silent, their lamps still spinning, shooting color into the mist and smoke. That kind of light always makes me think of death and destruction, the war at the end of the world. Maybe it's that color, that Martian orange. Artificial daylight. As if that's the kind of sun the survivors are going to see. My mood for fury died out with the fire. I began to shiver and said Adam, let's go in.

We didn't talk anymore that night, just went to sleep, but at breakfast he looked at me across the table and said So how did you lose him?

I freaked out, I said.

Then I repeated it, my voice getting louder and slower: I just freaked out, and if you don't leave me alone about it I'm going to freak out on you.

I threw my head forward and hid my face inside my hair, as if I was crying. Maybe I really was crying. Whatever, it was calculated. I wanted to divert him. He reached over and touched my cheek, got up and came closer, around the table, stood behind me rubbing my shoulders and my neck. He had good hands, broad and flat and healing. But as soon as I was calm again and looked at him, he smiled and said Tell me. You can tell me.

But what was there to tell? Sure, it was about a man, but who could take that kind of cause for serious, what with my history? It doesn't matter what set it off. It just happened. I'd drunk too much. I was upset. I lost control. It could happen to anybody. But when it happened to me, they called the police, they put me in Bridgewater, they took away my son.

So get him back, Adam said.

I can't, I said.

You can, he said, and when I came home at noon from swabbing toilets he'd called Barnstable County and found out everything I needed to know.

It wouldn't be hard, he told me, it wasn't impossible. He laughed. You drink too much, anyway, he said. We could go through it together. He'd go with me. I drink too much too, he said. All I had to do was demonstrate my good intentions. Be willing to work at it. Try to get healthy. Just try. Fill out some forms. Talk to a few people. He'd help me, he said. He wanted to help me.

I didn't answer for a while. I moved around the kitchen, washing dishes, throwing trash away, ignoring him. But finally I turned and said Don't you understand?

He was watching me, that innocent look on his face.

He's better off wherever he is, I said.

No, Adam said. You're his—

But I cut him short: Don't you understand yet? I don't want him. I didn't want him in the first place and I don't want him now.

Maybe it was true.

Adam just watched me like a stranger.

Well? I said.

He shrugged.

Well? I said again.

Nothing, he said. Then suddenly he broke: There are women in the world, he said, who die trying to find their missing children.

I thought he was going to cry. But when he got his breath back, he just said I don't believe you.

Believe it, I said.

I can't, he said.

That's your problem, I said.

Are we going to fight about this? he said.

Not if you leave it alone, I said.

I can't, he said.

You better think about that, I said. Think about it, I said. I'm going down and shoot some pool. You just sit here and think about it.

Don't go, he said.

I'll leave it alone, he said, and for a while he did. We didn't talk about Jesse anymore. I just always felt him there between us. We stopped fucking. We started fighting over money. It didn't happen all at once. There were still the mornings. Adam was always good in the mornings. He'd make the coffee. He'd bring it to me in bed. We'd lie around, just touching and playing. That's when I got to telling him my dreams. And he still had questions. He wanted to know about Bridgewater. What were those messages from the Devil and God?

Nothing, I said. Everything. Whatever I saw. Things I heard people say. Words on the radio, on TV. All contradictory. It won't do any good to repeat it.

Try me, he said.

But I was getting tired, tired of all the talking, all the words, I didn't want him to know. I wanted something to be left over that was mine. I'd say I couldn't remember. I'd say it didn't matter, it was nothing but insane. I made up examples, just to withhold the details I knew. Then suddenly

I'd realize that what I thought I was inventing was part of what was true. I made up a story about seeing another patient in a blood-red dress and silver slippers and thinking she was me, my image sent to me, and as soon as I told him, I knew it did happen, I did see a patient in a red dress and silver slippers and think she was my puppet, a puppet made of me, a doll someone wanted to stick pins in and confuse.

I didn't trust myself to speak to Adam anymore. I didn't want to call that back. I didn't want to remember the doctor dressed in black who came in from outside and told me he was an agent of the Devil, not in words but in his gestures, in his leer, in his offering ways out, ways to save my meal ticket—his phrase, not mine—ways to save my son.

I know now, knew telling Adam, that man was no doctor. He must have been a case worker or someone from the court. A perfectly ordinary well-meaning little man. But that wasn't how I saw him and it wasn't how I heard him and I didn't want to see or hear him again. Because only half of him was real and the other half scared me. It was just that drug they had me on to make me stop wanting booze—what it made me was crazy. But when I started telling Adam about the little doctor in the black suit, I hadn't remembered him yet. Like that girl in the red dress, I thought I was making him up. I thought I was making him up out of Adam, out of what Adam was doing to me with his endless insistence that I talk, his implicit plea that I straighten up and bring Jesse home, I thought I was making him up to tell Adam how I felt and to get him off my back. But suddenly I realized, right in the middle of telling it, that that little black-suited man had really been there, that I really had talked to him, that this doctor I was making up was somebody real. A guy from legal aid maybe, or from the county. Maybe he was the same guy that told Adam on the phone what I'd have to do. Where he came from doesn't matter. Because when I was in there, he was someone altogether different. His briefcase was the Devil's big black book. His pen was a knife and its ink was my blood. He wanted me to appeal for the return of my son. I wouldn't sign. He wanted my soul. No way, José. That's what I remembered. I said that out loud to Adam—No way, José—and suddenly I was breathing wild and deep and laughing out of control. Because I'd said those same words to that little man, over and over, laughing the same hysterical laugh, until they took me out of that conference room and tied me to my bed and sent the man away.

And when I finally stopped laughing, I stared at Adam across the table and sent him away too.

Maybe he didn't believe me at first. He never wanted to believe me. I moved him out of my bed onto Jesse's mattress in the living room, and still he didn't go. Then one morning I was going off to scrub toilets and change sheets and get rooms ready for Labor Day and I couldn't stand it anymore. I don't know what set me off. Maybe it was a dream I had, or some look on his face, or something he said. Maybe it was nothing, maybe he was just lying there smoking, or maybe he was still asleep. I remember seeing his shirt, a green sort of plaid and checked one, real thin, made of cotton. I remember it hanging over the back of one of the chairs, the one I usually sat in at the table. I remember the smell of it, Adam's smell. Maybe it was that, I don't know. But I stood in the open door, halfway gone, and screamed at him to get out, screamed he'd better be out by the time I came home because if he wasn't, one of us would be the victim of the season's last bloody crime.

He looked at me sadly. He never raised his voice. He said Is that what you really want?

That's what I really want, I said.

I left without closing the door.

Maybe I made myself ugly enough, I don't know. But when I came back after working all morning and drinking all day and into the night, Adam was gone. I'm not sure I realized it at first. I must have gone in to bed and passed out. I remember when I woke up in the morning wondering where I was. Then I saw. I was home. I didn't remember how I'd gotten there and Adam wasn't with me, but I was home.

It took me a few days to know he'd really left. I thought he was probably still knocking around town somewhere. But finally I understood. And I was glad. Life got easier. I don't know, I had some regrets maybe, maybe I did. Maybe I pined away for a while. I kept thinking about that Doors song, "L.A. Woman," and knowing that song was for me. Then Adam showed up out of nowhere early in December and I didn't even want to talk to him.

They'd found an old woman beaten to death that day. A couple of gay guys that lived downstairs from her had taken in a stranger, some vagrant kid from New York, and after three weeks living off them, the kid went upstairs to rob the old lady and when she caught him in the act he killed her with a hammer. Or at least that's what the police guess happened. Nobody knows.

I know one of the guys a little that gave that kid a place to stay. A real quiet guy, real nice.

Adam showed up that same night. It threw me to see him like that, just walking into the Bradford and coming over to me. I didn't even ask him where he'd been.

Let's go sit by the window, he said.

He bought me a drink.

Just get in? I said when we were facing each other.

Yeah, he said.

Hear what happened? I said.

I just got off the bus, he said.

So I told him about the bludgeoning.

You see where being good gets you? I said. Now those two nice, generous guys are going to spend the rest of their lives knowing they're responsible for that old woman's death.

Adam didn't say anything. I got up and went to the bar and got another two vodkas and went back and put his drink down in front of him. He looked up.

You don't want me here, do you? he said.

Not particularly, I said.

I guess I'll leave then, he said. I guess I'll look up a few old friends and then I'll leave.

Good luck, I said and walked away. I really didn't care.

He stuck around a day or two, maybe. I don't know. I never saw him again.

It's funny, though, now that he's really gone, something has disappeared. I keep reading about the homeless, and sometimes now I think I really am one of them, I should just go down to New York City and live on the sidewalk out of a plastic bag. Maybe in a few years, when I'm old and ugly and haven't got any choices left. I know what it looks like, what it sounds like when I say that. But I don't care. There's something I know now that I don't think I ever knew before: it's something I chose, this life, something I chose a long time ago, and even though what I really chose and what I thought I was choosing are two different things entirely, I made this bed and I'm willing to lie in it. And I am and always have been exactly what I want to be.

Spider

He has always liked spiders. He likes their webs, his favorite big and symmetrical—the spider, black and yellow, tiger-striped, poised at the center, waiting for its prey. On the farm when he was little he would search for days to find a web in progress, a web not quite begun. He found only finished ones. They sprang up overnight, in the daisies, in the chrysanthemums. Every morning he stared at them transfixed. When a fly landed—a ladybug, a beetle, a mosquito, a spitball he'd toss into it, a fleck of soil, a seed—the web shuddered, the spider scurried, ate what it found there or spun it up in silk or spat it away. At night, in the bedroom he shared with Rainy and any visiting child who stayed a while and left, he conjured the scent of chrysanthemums and imagined the work of spiders out on the land. He marveled that the spider, a creature vulnerable to gravity, threw itself without hesitation into empty space, into the fall. In the jerk of sleep, he was himself the falling spider. It leaped. It leaped again. Behind every flight, it left a trail. Four long threads made the axes of its weaving, and in the morning, at the center of a web shimmering with dewdrops, he found the spider waiting: eight legs listening to eight live wires of dew-silvered silk.

Rainy wouldn't go near them. She believed what one of those visiting children had told her: tiger spiders spit poison in your eye.

He was glad she was afraid of them. He watched the spiders alone.

It was only later that he learned the spider's silk served also as a parachute, the leaping spider didn't fall. By then he had secretly decided he was one of them, and knew that when the time came, like the spider he would leap and soar and fly away.

For too long, every day had been the same. His mother sent money, he dealt a little dope. In summers he sold popcorn at the movies. He lay awake most nights, slept through the mornings, and in the afternoons hung out with little girls. We had always been his friends, his sisters. Because of Rainy. You girls are too young for me, he told us when we flirted. I'm your brother, I protect you from guys like me. Jane used to laugh, and Rainy and I shared glances. He had noticed my December Woman. He was hanging out in bars. He played pinball, videogames, pool, drank beer and chatted with the chess and backgammon players, learned the names of the hangers-on and regulars, learned December Woman's name and the names and faces of her friends. His face became familiar to her too, she talked at him sometimes, saying nothing special, and in his sleep he listened to her slurred husky voice. When she freaked out behind the bar of the Bradford, he stared at those eyes and saw his mother and couldn't move.

It was March last year when he told me his name wasn't Dylan anymore, his name was Spider now and don't forget it. We were sitting close together on a green wooden bench in the center of town, on the place called the meat rack where in summer all day long and into the night, especially late when the bars are closed, men pick up other men. Mama was working across the street. I saw her now and then, moving in and out of sight in big panes of glass. The sun was going down. The day was clouded over. I felt the angle of the light change. A chill came into the air. I asked him why he wanted a new name. Behind us, where benches line the walk to the Town Hall steps, a little boy chased pigeons and two old ladies in black coats shouted to each other in Portuguese across the open square. His eyes were fixed on his feet, his legs stretched out long in front of him. He didn't look up when he answered. He was two years old when Rainy was born, he said. His mother was her mother's midwife and his mother's hands were the first to hold her. With the baby in her arms, she knelt down beside him and he pressed his tiny fingers to Rainy's red new wrinkled skin.

Now I live in an empty room above a store, he said. My name is Spider now, I don't love my mother's heroes, and I don't believe in magic.

When I asked him that day on the meat rack why he wanted a new name, he told me Dylan was someone else's name, he wanted a name that was his own, but in April when Katie Roberts came back from Bridgewater and asked the same question, he told her, Because I have eight legs, and grabbed her bare arms laughing. Like a nursery rhyme, Spider, Spider, what's inside her? repeated in his ears, and he looked at her steadily and saw she would let him learn. His quarter was up for pool, the guy who'd won the game before was calling, and Spider didn't know how to drag himself out of those eyes. Play, she told him finally, I'm not going anywhere, but when his game was over, she was down at the end of the bar talking to Adam, radiant as a dream.

Eight months later, in early December, Adam came back to town. Spider saw him in the Bradford, with Katie Roberts. He saw Katie walk away. He sat up all night at his window, watching the street, and at dawn he saw Adam again and he went down. He couldn't tell where he had come from. Maybe he'd slept on the beach under the landing where the wharf rats slept when the weather was warm. Maybe he'd found a friend. Just looking at him—rumpled, unshaven, dragging his feet—Spider knew he hadn't spent the night with Katie. He followed him to the Hyannis bus. He followed him on. The bus was almost empty. He took the seat across the aisle from where Adam sat. He started a conversation. It was easy. An old woman had just been killed by some transient kid from the city. The kid hadn't been found yet. Spider talked about the crime. Adam asked how long he'd lived in town and Spider said three years, he came up from Brooklyn when his mom was drinking so much she couldn't handle him in the house. He said he was done with school now, his mom was better and wanted him to come home, but he couldn't make himself go. He was waiting for something, he said. He didn't know what. Adam asked who his friends were, if he had pictures. Do you know Tess? he said.

Oh, Tess, sure, Spider said, I have a picture of Tess, and he went for his wallet and pulled it out, one of those posed school pictures from the year before.

Then Adam laughed and said, For a minute, I thought it was you.

Me? Spider said.

The old woman, Adam said. He said it laughing, like he knew he was a fool.

Holding Spider's picture of me (wearing a white sweater, hair long and loose around my shoulders, embarrassed wide-mouthed grin on my face), looking at it a long time, then up and out the window as the bus drew into Wellfleet, Adam told him he'd meant to see my mother.

Her mother? Spider said. I thought you went with that Katie Roberts.

You know her too? He reached into a pocket of his army jacket, took out a pint of vodka, and lifted it in offering. It wasn't even seven-thirty yet. Spider refused.

I meant to, Adam said.

Tess's Mama? Holly?

Tell her hello, Adam said. He drank from the bottle. Go into Rags and Roses and tell her Adam says hello.

Something seemed to occur to him. He glanced up at the empty luggage rack above Spider's seat. Then he sank back into the photograph.

Spider didn't want to lose him like that. He'd followed him to talk to him, to get him to talk. He didn't even know about what.

Anything else? he asked. Anything else I can tell her?

Adam didn't answer him. Instead he said, The important things, you know. The important things can't be photographed.

They're always crummy, Spider said, those school pictures, and knew as he was saying it this wasn't what Adam meant.

The whole conversation went that way. Adam drank, looked at my picture, said something off the wall, and Spider missed it every time. As soon as he was answering, he knew.

Then suddenly on Christmas Eve, Katie Roberts pulled him into a corner and before he understood what was happening he was following her red velvet thighs up his stairs. He was a baby, drunk with eggnog and bourbon and beer, mistletoe and holly and fantasy coming true. By the time she finished telling him her story, the candle stuck in the beer bottle on his orange-painted table had burned down to nothing, the rush had left his body, and the day was rising blue. She hadn't even kissed him. But he was touched. She had given him her wasted life.

On Christmas Eve, she picked him out of a crowd, and in six weeks he learned more from her than he ever wanted to know: how to fuck, how to use his hands, his fingers, his tongue, how to wake a woman in the middle of the night, how to exhaust her capacity for pleasure, how to use a woman up, how to lose caring, how to get sick from too much satisfaction, how to know disgust at the center of desire, how a life ended early that narrowed its excitements and burned them up, how waste was not romantic, how loss was not perceptive, how poverty was boring, how magic was a lie, how one wrong thing would always lead to another, how accumulation was carnivorous, how a history solidified and a life became an object, how death kept on breathing, how blank her beautiful eyes were, how decayed her faithless skin, how futile was conjecture, how the world killed the spirit, that we were not his sisters, that I was hiding in his dreams, that greed had its virtues, that he might as well buy into what the system had to offer, because there was no way to buy himself out.

I was alone on the meat rack waiting for Rainy and Jane when December Woman walked up and stopped in front of me and spoke to me by name. It was Saturday. It was February. A wind was blowing. She was wearing black boots. She hugged her sealskin coat around her body. She said, I want to talk to you. Friday night's mascara was smeared around her eyelids. Her lips were white. Her cheeks were red. She sat down. She smelled of sweet perfume.

She said, You think you know me, don't you?

She laughed at my confusion.

She said, Spider tells me you girls are interested in magic. He thinks you'd like to see my cards, you'd like your fortunes told. He says you're extraordinary girls. He talks about you all the time.

She laughed. She stood up. She said, Spider will show you the way.

If there had been a fog, she would have vanished into it. She went to him and said, I want to see that girl today.

The evening before, when Mama and Blue came in with the mail, she had a letter from Adam. She didn't open it. She put it on the table where I sat doing homework. She waited for Blue to leave. The letter was postmarked from Santa Fe. Mama put a tape on my player and turned the volume loud. She looked like she wanted to dance. Handel's Water Music boomed out from the little speakers. Blue took off. Mama picked up her letter and went to her room. When she came back, she stood behind me and asked what I wanted to eat. I told her to stop working, she didn't have to be a waitress twenty-four hours a day, and she laughed and wrapped her arms around me and put her chin down on my head.

So Adam's coming back to New York, she said. The trumpets sounded on the tape. So what shall we eat?

Two hours later she was still goofing on something, dancing around to the Rolling Stones while she washed the dishes, when Blue telephoned from town. She hesitated. I watched her face. She almost didn't go. Now he was probably sleeping in her bed, or waking up there, smoking, looking at the ceiling. Her letter was on the dresser. I saw it in my mind, framed by the chipped green paint.

The last perfect autumn day before the weather turned to winter we had walked into the beech forest—Spider, me, Rainy, Jane. The air was cold and clean, the leaves and trunks and branches haloed, as blinding as the sun. We climbed the tree in the hollow, so big and ancient and unlike the others we never knew what kind it was. We jumped off its heavy branches. We yelled when we rolled in its crisp new-fallen leaves. That February morning, alone on the meat rack after Katie Roberts spoke to me, I saw Spider yelling, jumping from that tree. He never would do it again. Maybe I never would either. Every aging step in him was an aging step in me. He was four years older but that didn't affect the pattern. When Rainy worried he was turning black, magic came at me. When he changed his name to Spider and mooned after December Woman, as soon as she took him to bed I began to bleed. On Christmas Eve, she'd picked him out of a crowd. Now he was in her service and she had sent him out for me.

She waited at her kitchen table. She drank coffee, smoked cigarettes, fingered her deck of cards. Vague white light came in through her crocheted curtains. The room was warm. The oven door was open, the gas was on. The ashtray in front of her was full when we got there. She reminded me of Mama, sitting in the hanging smoke.

Think of Alice in Wonderland, I want to say to Spider now: You're nothing but a pack of cards. Think of Katie Roberts, going crazy behind the Bradford bar. Think of yourself, following Adam to Hyannis because he'd been the lover of a woman you hardly knew. Think of Mama, feeding her addiction to China Blue's body, all the while telling him she loves another man. Think of Katie again, playing fortuneteller in her kitchen for reasons none of us can guess. Remember yourself, leaning back against her sink, watching the girls you used to protect fall under her spell. Remember her voice, going distant, trance inducing, strange. Remember me, then, I want to say. And again: Remember me.

Study each card carefully, the fortuneteller says. Each position has a meaning. Each card has a meaning, based on traditional symbols, modified by position and the other cards that appear. Pay attention to what's pictured. The established meanings are only clues. Let the images act on you like dreams. What matters is what you see.

From where Spider stands the cards are only sounds, soft whisperings while I shuffle, clicks under Katie's nails. He can't see the images, only the back of Katie's head, Rainy's and Jane's profiles, my blank attentive face.

This is the card that covers you, the fortuneteller says. *This card represents the problem, your question.*

The Two of Swords, reversed, she says. *A card of dilemma, a card of paralysis, a card of refusing to see.*

She turns up another. It clicks against the first.

This is the card that crosses you. This is the obstacle you have to overcome.

The Devil, she says. *Desire. All desire that chains you to the flesh, all flesh that binds you to the earth.*

He is listening for the method in this game. He is listening for its motive. She turns up another card.

The card that supports you. The card that defines your lower horizon.

The Queen of Wands, she says.

This card is your mother.

The room is growing darker, the day clouding over. Spider sees my face more clearly as the window light goes dim. He watches my eyes move with the rhythms of the fortuneteller's voice: down to the new card, up to the fortuneteller's eyes.

She lays out another card.

Your upper horizon, she says. *Together these cards form your limits. Not absolutely, but for today. The boundaries of this region of the landscape of your life.*

The Ace of Pentacles. Reversed, the pentagram, the Devil's sign. Reversed, a card of repression. You have secrets you are forced to conceal.

She turns up another card.

The card that follows behind you. The card of the recent past.

The Lovers reversed. Card of exile. Card of the Fall. In the recent past you began to know. You resist with all that's in you. But once you begin to know, you never can stop knowing.

Another: *The immediate future,* she says. *The Knight of Swords. A card of impetuous action, not necessarily your own. A card of anger and impulse and change. A card of breaking away.*

She lays out another card.

Your inner awareness, she says. *The Nine of Swords. The card of nightmares.*

And another: *Your outer being. The card of your promise. The card of your presence in the world.*

The Ace of Cups, she says. *Five waterfalling streams: life, grace, the word, joy, the law.*

And again: *Your hopes and fears. The King of Swords.*

She stops. We all feel her stopping.

This is a man, she says. *A particular man.*

You know who this man is, she says, her eyes fixed on me.

She turns up another card.

The card of eventual outcome. The Eight of Swords reversed. The bonds fall away. The swords fall away. The card of release from false bondage. Exile's return.

The fortuneteller's breath stops. Spider can almost hear her counting, until Rainy breaks the silence.

It's China Blue, she says.

What? Katie says, her voice her own again.

That King, Jane says. It's China Blue. Her mother's boyfriend.

Katie turns back to me: my face still, my eyes open wider and wider.

In that look we share a secret the rest of them can't see.

Spider, Katie calls suddenly. More vodka, she says and when he brings it she says, Look at these cards.

As if he understands her. As if he'll know what they mean.

One hot summer morning on the farm, Spider and Rainy were

spraying each other with water from the big garden hose when they got the idea to make a swimming pool. The dirt was rich and soft and easy to dig with their toy buckets and a shovel he got from the shed, and when they got too hot from the work they sprayed each other and took off their frayed shorts cut from last winter's blue jeans and discovered how the mud they made clung to their skin and kept them cool. The grownups on the place were mostly asleep, but after a while music from the cabin down the hill told them Zack was up, maybe working already, making shelves, a table, chairs. When the hole was deep and round enough for their two little bodies they put the hose in and watched the clear water turn a thin murky brown. Together they hesitated, stepping in, but when their feet stirred up the dark soil at the bottom they knew what to do: squatting, they loosened the earth and mixed it, turning the hose in only when they needed more liquid, until the mud was thick and swallowed them up to their necks and they both had room to lie back against the sides, their legs out straight and lazily kicking. When they heard music from the kitchen they knew Rainy's mother was up and saw Peaches come out on the rambling porch and stretch his body at the day. They held their breath and waited for him to see them and when he turned away to go in they wiggled in their tadpole bath and giggled and waved and yelled his name until he came down and took off his jeans and got in and dug the hole bigger and deeper. When Zack came up from the cabin he stopped and laughed at the sight of them, sunlight glancing off his polished-copper hair, and when he came out again from the house he was carrying a beer, and Rainy's mother and Joe and Priscilla came after him and they all stripped off their clothes and laughed and scrubbed each other with mud and packed it onto their faces and wallowed as happily as Spider and Rainy did. Lorna joined them next and squealed climbing in, holding her hair up on her head with both hands, until she had to let it go. Spider's mother came out last, reluctant, but Zack said bring a six-pack and she did and then she took off her clothes and climbed in too.

Rainy was the first to get tired of it and Spider got out with her, and as they stood there rinsing off, their glittering little bodies pink and cold and clean, suddenly it was funny, looking down at the muddy grownups, Rainy's mother so fat and Zack so thin, and Priscilla letting the mud dry on her neck and face, her eyes closed against the sun. Then Lorna sent them in for towels and one by one the grownups followed them out, finishing their beers, talking about breakfast, lounging on the grass to let the mud bake or rinsing off with the hose, and Joe on the porch steps singing and playing his banjo.

Zack and Spider's mother were the last to leave the mud bath and when they stood up together, the mud in his red beard, his pale face so wet and brown and only the eyes bright, like some soldier in a jungle, Spider saw him look at her—not at her breasts or her belly, not at her nakedness, but right at her, into her eyes—and saw Zack's cock swell under its slick brown coating and saw his mother see it. He watched them go to the hose and rinse each other off and saw the water gleam on Zack's pale freckled skin. He gave them towels and watched them pick up their clothes and walk down the path to Zack's cabin through a radiance of yellow leaves, and remembering the yellow butterflies he'd seen on a road once, driving with Zack and Joe, swarming yellow butterflies so dense Zack slowed the jeep to a crawl and made him get out and shoo them away so they wouldn't die on the radiator, Spider led Rainy back to their mudhole and added water and mixed it again and climbed back in, and it didn't occur to either of them that grownups weren't the same kind of children they were or that age and time could bring anything but more abundant satisfactions—as if they were children in some remote paradise instead of in the country that had just put a man on the moon, as if on their dropped-out farm near Woodstock they already knew what they would be part of a few weeks later when with half a million others like Zack and Spider's mother and Peaches and Priscilla and Rainy's mother and Lorna and Joe they would declare themselves outlaws in the eyes of America—a nation outside the nation that was napalming a fertile land, bombing an ancient city, destroying a proud people, and tear-gassing, clubbing, and imprisoning its own; as if they couldn't imagine that within a few years they all would scatter, find themselves cities to live in, do time in hospitals, psych wards, jails—retreat, regroup, Rainy and her mother to Provincetown, Zack down to the Florida Keys where maybe he's still building that boat, and Spider and his mother alone to Brooklyn, to a neighborhood full of street-corner men and air that smelled like gym sweat.

When he looks at the cards on Katie's table, all in an instant, brighter than when it was happening, that day in the mud and the brilliant liquid sun in yellow leaves is what Spider sees.

Because this happens to him, he understands what happens to me.

I close my eyes. A narrow wind howls down the walks between the buildings, and out of her silence Mama says, You know, sometimes you feel how precarious this town is.

We stop what we're doing separately and listen together to the storm. Rain rattles the windows, the rising tide batters the bulkheads and pilings.

As if that water, Mama says, could suck the sand out from under everything.

As if we're on the border, she says, the frontier, all the waters of the earth one living creature, collapsing continents, coming slowly, eating everything away.

I'm three. I'm walking with Mama along the beach in Santa Cruz. I make her hold my hand and won't let my feet get wet. I hold on tight when a wave comes in, trying to pull her back to the safe sand. But Mama, brave and little beside it, kicks the ocean.

Then China Blue stands me up against the wall.

I look at Katie and I look at Spider.

I forgot, I say.

I made myself forget, and then I really forgot.

I think we should go, Rainy says. I think we all should go now.

I turn to Katie, pleading: I forgot. Don't you understand me?

But you didn't, Katie says. You can't forget. There's nothing you can forget. Forgetting isn't possible.

Rainy's right, Jane says. We better go.

No, I say. I'm not ready. I tell them to leave.

You're sure you're all right here? Rainy asks.

Of course I'm all right, I say and I feel like a traitor and I don't care.

Rainy and Jane were gone. I couldn't look at Spider. I couldn't look at Katie. I spoke, when I spoke, with my eyes closed. I didn't want to lose what Katie had given back to me. I drank tea while she drank vodka. Eventually I opened my eyes. We sat there, the three of us, at her table the rest of the afternoon, and Katie listened with a cloudy, thoughtful gaze and drank and asked me questions. Spider was silent. He didn't want to believe me. But what he wanted didn't matter.

Last April Mama loved two men. Almost a year later, she loves them still.

If both chose her at the same time, she wouldn't know what to do. She reads the Bible, methodically, chapter by chapter and book by book. With friends like Mason she's a different person. She's tough, she makes jokes, she laughs at the end of the world. At the restaurant she's efficient. She's good to everyone but sometimes gets jumpy, snaps, fights back. She doesn't take shit but she makes too many allowances. She cares about people. Even strangers. Even strangers can hurt her. Sometimes she breaks, goes into a corner and cries. She believes she's not a secret person because her face shows what she's feeling. Her face does show what she's feeling—her voice shows it too—but she is a secret person just the same. Most people don't understand her, no matter what she reveals. She's braver than she knows. I love my Mama. I love China Blue.

She takes on the colors of her lovers. Their characteristics, their gestures, their tones of voice. Like her, I began to learn. If she picks up the manners of her lovers, she always returns to herself. After they're gone, she makes them into friends. Some barrier dissolves. She absorbs them. Like her, I drew a circle around myself. I had put China Blue out somewhere beyond it. When he came near, he would be somebody else.

Mama, I said one day that spring, and then I said something silly but what I wanted to say was in the winter I used to dream about China Blue, I guess they were dreams, I don't know, Mama, what was it I knew?

For a month or more he was gone, and then when I saw him on the street he bought me an ice cream at Spiritus, just re-opened for the season. While other kids played Space Invaders, we sat in a booth and talked, and when I told him to come see Mama sometime, he said he had but she wasn't home, he'd look for her again, and it was not the China Blue who had come to me those nights in the winter.

Who was it then? I wanted to know, and Jane said Forget it, or What was it like? depending on her mood, and the more I told her the less I remembered really, in my body or my skin. When Rainy found us talking about it, she said it was magic, You'd better not even talk about it, if you keep talking about it something'll get you for it, and Jane laughed and said it didn't happen, Nothing happened, Tess just dreamed it all, it's not even magic, Rainy, it's only dreams, but Rainy said Then how come she knows so much? and nobody had any answers, no one could think what to say.

Mama, I wanted to ask, tell me about this, what it is, but I couldn't because it was April and Mama was in love and for once I thought maybe Mama wouldn't know.

Mama's new love confused her. Her love confused me.

Adam was her friend when we lived in New York, not her lover. Her work took more of her attention there. She didn't have so much time for lovers then, or even for me. She had boyfriends now and then, but they didn't last, and each day when she finished at work and picked me up from child care or school, she didn't go off roaming or leave me alone at home. We had an ordinary life together there, like other mothers and kids, and she had hers and I had mine.

I sat at the table drawing. Mama sat at the window smoking and listened to the room. There was a hum. For a long time, only the hum. There was a drop of water, from the faucet into the sink. There was a voice, from the street, not meant for her. There was a car, not stopping. It was really April then. Suddenly. Boards came off the windows of shops and houses. Carpenters were working all over town. Everything got warm outside. Mama listened to the hum. Something squeaking. Footsteps upstairs. The gate in the driveway next door. In love with Adam, she became so silent, so still. As if she was always waiting. Not impatiently. Just sitting the way she did then, in her wicker chair by the window, not talking, not reading, not doing anything I could see.

I was drawing a sea beast, his big blue eyes, inventing him while I drew: He lived deep in the water. A dolphin, a whale. The Loch Ness monster maybe. Now and then he came up for air, made tidal waves, earthquakes, unnatural catastrophes. Then he withdrew. He was only human. Drifting in his own sea. Swim out there with him, I told myself. You can't float. You lose your bearings. You think you're at the center of yourself. You think yourself is what you know. You're swimming blind and think some mystery is in process of revealing. But he doesn't want company. The water's his. He is the water and brought you here to let you drown.

I liked Adam, I had always liked Adam, and I liked to see Mama happy, the way she was with him and after he'd gone, and even though Adam was nothing like China Blue—he was in Mama's world and I could see it, grownup, alien and withheld from me, not on the surface, but inside—even so, I caught some of her excitement and I was happy around him, easy, simple and funny, almost a child again. Maybe Mama felt that way too. Washed clean. As if China Blue never was. Not even a shadow. Not really a dream. More like a fear, like walking home late on Commercial Street with no one around, no voices, no footsteps, a possibility ahead or off to the side, a sudden voice, sudden footsteps that come from nowhere, that you become aware of and listen to, that pass you by or turn away and let you breathe again in the night.

Adam was all presence, like the silence itself, or the water—just there— and the Blue who bought me an ice cream was just Blue, another person, someone I knew who was always telling me to listen to newer music, Elvis Costello, the Pretenders, Talking Heads, not just the Beatles and Stones, who was funny sometimes and laughed at my stories and liked my friends, who was almost a boy himself again and whose hands had never touched me in the dark.

He appeared in the window, walking up the deck stairs. He tapped on the glass. Mama waved, and the cat followed him in. Mama smiled without getting up. She offered him a beer.

Sure, he said as if he didn't really want it and went to the refrigerator and brought out two.

I've been looking for work, he said. I drove around and parked in restaurant parking lots.

He glanced over at me. He asked if he could see my drawing.

Sure, I said. I could feel him over my shoulder. I didn't want him standing behind me looking. I don't like it much, I said.

It's nice, he said. But *nice* isn't what he saw.

You want to come up one of these days, he said to Mama when he was leaving, it's another month before I move.

The high horizon. The flattening of everything you see. Rainy said she was a sea witch, or wanted to be. We were sitting on the breakwater, our legs dangling down the rocks. The weather kept changing. A sea witch, Rainy said, is a witch that sells weather. They lived here, she said. They traded with fishermen and sailors. She untied knots in her magic cord. She sold them good winds.

Along the curving harbor the town stood small and etched in stone, the water the same flat slate as the sky. A figure on the beach, a tall man, gradually approached us, stopping now and then to pick something up—a bottle, broken glass, a piece of plastic, a shell, a rock, a bone. He could have been finding pipe stems, made of clay, or fragments of clay dolls, or a whole one—old things lost at sea and buried, pulled up with every tide.

Rainy's puppy splashed, chasing seagulls at the waterline. The tide was out, and so low we could have walked across the mudflats to Long Point in channels no deeper than our knees.

I think that man out there is Adam, I said, and I watched him wander, toward us and away. Everything he gathered he held in one hand to examine. Then he looked out at the water or the sky and dropped what he was holding back to the sand. Sometimes he just stopped, not picking up anything, and for a while he turned and walked backward, facing the town. I said again, I think that's Adam. Mama's in love with him, I said.

In love? Rainy said. What about China Blue?

I shrugged. I said Mama's known Adam a long time. I said Mama's boyfriends come and go.

But Mama was at Blue's.

She told him how she sat home listening, not telling him the reason, and they sat together on his floor and listened to birds. He laughed a minute and said it sounded like some machine was out there cranking up bird sounds. She told him what she heard from her window: the cars, the footsteps, the gate, the squeaking. She said the squeaking was her favorite because she didn't know what it was. He thought a moment, then laughed and said, I like that. When she got home, someone had been there but she found no signs. On the street she had run into me and Rainy but it was not our presence she felt in those rooms. The apartment was empty. She was alone. Even the cat was out, sitting on the deck, glancing in the window, at the water, at birds with his great placid yellow eyes. The sun was bright again and seagulls were wading the edge of the water. The tide was low. The cat saw something to chase and ran for the garbage bins.

A few days later Mama turned thirty-five, and Blue came by and took her for a ride. They left before sunset and it got so late and dark I could see my face in her window. I didn't like to think of them driving up the Cape, some tape playing loud, high beams on the road, red taillights ahead of them, leading them into the night. I studied my reflection in the window and almost saw her there instead of me. When we lived in New York, the guy that lived downstairs from us knocked on the door one day and asked me was my sister home. Mama was good at her work in New York, she knew she was good, but she didn't like it. She wanted something real. Real, she said all the time. Real, she says over and over, till you almost don't know what the word means. It's the reason we're always moving. Or the reason we stay. It's the reason she left my dad, when I was little. It's always somehow the reason: She wants *something* to be real, or something to be *more* real, or something to be *real*. I wouldn't have minded leaving again. We've never left anywhere we never went back to. We always make new friends. We always see our old ones. We never lose anything. We just get bigger and bigger. Like my face there, out beyond the glass, almost as big as Mama's, floating in the night.

You don't exist, I thought to him. You don't exist, you don't exist, you don't exist.

I was trying to draw unicorns but couldn't concentrate, couldn't control my pen. I put down the pen I was holding, a red one for the band of rainbow I was about to make. I looked at the pens spread around the table, down at the purple one my foot was rolling on the floor.

My unicorn had hazel eyes. I'd given him black lashes, a red rose between his teeth. His eyes were sad. I didn't like the drawing. I didn't know why. I crumpled it up.

You don't exist, I said, out loud because Mama wasn't home to hear. I went very still. I'll make you not exist, I thought. Nothing ever happened. You never were.

My belly opened, a balloon blowing up. *You don't exist*. The swelling feeling scared me. My head began to ache. I clutched a pen, a blue one, and breathed with the swelling. What scared me was it almost worked. For five seconds I felt it: He did not exist. Then my head ached and I clutched the dark blue pen, shook my head, and stopped the thing I knew I'd almost done.

I see Mama. She has a cigarette in her hand. She quit for six months and then in winter smoked four or five a night, whenever she was out and could bum them. She repaid everyone with packs until when Adam came she sat at that table smoking and drinking vodka with him all one Saturday and started buying packs of her own. Two weeks later, he's left her, backed off, saying it was all too heavy, and she sits in her wicker chair with the big floral print in pink on navy cushions, holding a cigarette and watching the smoke rise. Alone beside her window, she hears the water plash against the pilings, the sand. She hears foghorns. A dog barks. A car passes. A question hangs in the air. Everything stops and between question and answer the pause is infinite. China Blue is invisible and with him someone else, who exists in absence and silence, whose face is her face and not hers, and about whom nothing she knows will ever be said.

A few days before I left town for summer with my dad, I ran in the beech forest, on my way to meet Rainy and Jane. A sweet smell was in the air and steam almost visible rising from the earth. I saw myself from outside: running the dusty trail, a long-legged girl in a faded purple T-shirt and short white denim overalls. My hair blew out behind me, and I was damp at my forehead, my shoulders, the back of my neck. I was too big for my body. Too big for my body I didn't fit inside my skin. I tore a branch from a scrub pine. I ran until I saw our tree and threw myself off the path, rolling to the roots in the old dead leaves.

Blue, Blue, I said, flat on my back, it didn't happen. He never was my China Blue. I made him up. Like magic. Like Mama said.

Rainy's puppy was the first to find me, his big puppy feet padding onto my belly, his tongue hot on my cheek, his rope tickling my hands where it dangled free behind. Rainy stood over me laughing, then Jane came asking What are you doing? Why do you look sad?

Nothing, I told them. Blue's coming back to my mother, I think. I think he's coming back, and for a moment I felt him again, inside me, my body swimming lavender.

It never happened, I said. I think Jane was right.

You know what it is to be imprisoned? Adam asked Spider on that bus six months later. Subjugated, tyrannized? This, he said, pinching the flesh of his arm. This, shaking his bottle. That, opening his hand toward the world outside the window. You can't stop anything. Things just go on and on. People get tied up in the fetal position and hung upside down by their thumbs and toes until they die. You can't photograph it. Even if they permit you, you can't photograph it. Only the bodies. And the bodies are only bodies and the bodies don't count. The most you can do is refuse to live in the privileged world. And that's not enough.

I grew up on talk like that, Spider said and knew right away it wasn't the same.

You don't know you know, Adam said. But you will. Everyone knows, sooner or later, he said, and went on talking, rambling, one thing following another like signs along the highway.

In her kitchen Katie said to me, Adam wrote to your mother, and for half a second I thought she really was a witch.

China Blue told me, she said. Last night.

I fell inside, like the figures in the cards. I went cold, like air, as if air was rushing through me.

You know him, too? I said.

She laughed, not unkindly. I know everyone, she said.

You don't know my mother, I said.

Because I don't choose to know your mother, she said.

The air inside me froze. I turned to Spider for help. He wouldn't meet my eyes. I turned back to Katie, fighting tears.

I love my mother, I said.

Lucky you, she said. Some of us don't. She smiled. Her smile was radiant. I remembered she was full of vodka.

My bottom lip was trembling.

I'm cold inside, I said. Could I have more tea? and it was Spider who got up and went to the stove and turned the water on to boil.

I don't much like mothers, Katie said. I'm sorry. I didn't mean to hurt you about her.

I nodded, biting my lips together.

Still friends? she said.

I shrugged. I lowered my head and hid in my hair. I said, It's not just that.

Of course not, she said. I looked up at her again. She smiled.

It was easier forgetting, I said. I'm scared now to go home to them. There was a reason to forget.

There's nothing to be scared of except forgetting, she said. The rest doesn't matter.

How do you know that? I asked her and she said she had to learn it, someone had to teach her.

Adam? I said, and the kettle hissed, and looking through me like that stranger riding roller skates in the night she said, I think it's time for you to go.

I walked home in twilight. I watched for stars but none came out. I lingered on the deck a while, looking at the water. When I went in, Mama was getting ready to go out with Blue. They were eating at Cookie's she said and seeing the early movie at the Crown & Anchor, did I want to come?

No, I said, I was tired, I had homework to do.

I brought some books to the table and made myself busy until Blue came in. When he sat down beside me, I smelled soap, cologne, shampoo. Something sweet and clean, almost packaged but not quite fresh, already his. A damp lock of hair curled at his neck. He lit a cigarette. His fingers were long. His wrists were bony. He kept his leather jacket on.

Mama was in the kitchen, organizing dinner for me.

Aren't you coming, Tess? he asked.

I shook my head.

I watched his eyes, so brown and green.

Put those books away, why don't you? he said. Come with us.

I shook my head. He was not my mother's lover. I was not a little girl. I stood up and left the room. I lay down on my bed and put my elbow over my eyes. Mama followed me, asking was something wrong. My face still hidden, I told her no, I was only tired, I'd probably go to bed early.

Okay, then, she said. I guess we're leaving. She was looking at me funny, I could tell.

Have a good time, I said before she closed the door.

Later that night Spider and Katie were standing at the bar in the Governor Bradford when he turned away from their conversation and saw Mama and Blue playing chess at a table near the window. He stared at Blue's skinny face. He crossed the room.

At first they didn't notice.

He hovered, a rage building, a memory, Katie's sloppy wet decay, her dry-eyed history, my fear, a look in my eyes as hungry as Katie's, the cold hilarity after I'd gone, Katie crying *Bingo!* as if he knew what she was after, and he did, and tackled her, took her on the floor, a smell of me and the outdoors still hanging in the room.

Suddenly Mama looked up from the chessboard, surprised. She knew Spider's face but not his name.

How can you sit there?—the words broke out of him as soon as she showed him her eyes.

What? she said.

He might have hesitated. He might have thought about me. But he was already in it.

Don't you know what this man's done? he said. How can you sit there? and she looked at him, at Blue, and back at Spider and said, I think you'd better go.

And he: No, lady, Holly, Tess's Mama, you'd better listen because I'm going to tell you what Tess never will.

And she (slowly, remembering a mystery): What?

Speak up, he told her. You want to listen? You want me to tell you, Tess's Mama? You better want it, Tess's Mama, because you're going to have to hear it because, Tess's Mama, you are blind.

Then Blue, impatient: Ignore him, Holly—the kid is drunk.

Spider leaned close to their table then, his lips at her ear.

This man, he said, this man here, your boyfriend China Blue, this man fucked your daughter.

He stood up straight again, looking down at him—Blue impassive, deaf, dumb, back stiff, already standing, grabbing his jacket, turning to Mama.

Did you hear? Spider asked him, shouting in his face—did you think nobody knew? and the rage breaking, scattered, and laughing suddenly he walked away.

Let's go, Blue said to Mama. Come on.

But Mama didn't move.

He turned and pushed himself out the door. She didn't move. He passed by the window, hands rammed deep in his pockets, taking long strides, eyes to the ground. Still she didn't move. Spider and Katie watched her from the bar. Blue didn't come back. She finished her drink slowly and slowly she walked out. Thinking: *This is not what I'm supposed to do*. The night was cold. The air was wet. She could feel the snow coming. She didn't believe what Spider had told her. She didn't disbelieve it. It immobilized her while she watched Blue go. It dragged her while she walked, and her bootsteps sounding questions—*What? What? What?*—pulled her home.

Tess, she whispered, waking me up. Tess.

She was in my room. Sitting on the floor, close to my head.

Mama? I said.

Tell me, she said.

Tell you? I said. What, Mama?

Blue, she said. Your friend, she said.

And then I knew.

I looked for her eyes in the darkness.

I don't know, I said. Mama, I don't know, and she held me in her arms and pressed her face against my hair.

Tell me, she said again.

I was confused. I never meant for her to hear it. I was angry that he'd told her, but when I felt her broad, strong hand on my head and she said again, Tell me, for an instant I really thought I would.

Then she said, Tess. Tess, this can't be true.

I let her hold me. I let her stroke my hair.

I don't know, Mama, I said finally. In the morning, I said. Mama, in the morning.

She sat with me a long time. I curled up into my covers and tried to go back to sleep. After a while I just pretended, until I heard her leave the room. I listened while she made a drink. I listened while she let the cat in. I heard her sit down at the table, smoking a cigarette, the ice cubes clinking in her glass. I heard the sound of paper shuffling. She was looking at my homework maybe, or reading her letter from Adam again. I heard her go into her bedroom. I heard her shut the door. I listened a long time. Then I got out of bed and put my clothes on. In stocking feet, I went into the other room. Out the window I saw snow falling. On the table, Adam's letter lay open next to her glass. I picked up her purse and opened the wallet and took out seventy dollars, leaving some ones and a ten. I folded her letter back into its envelope and took it to my room and closed the door. I put my jacket on and zipped the letter and the money into the pockets. I pulled my boots on. Off my room there was an entry hall and a door to the street. We never used that door. We almost forgot it was there. The hall was piled with suitcases and empty boxes from the last time we moved. I went into that hallway and out and walked in the blue-white glitter the streetlamps made of the falling snow. Deeper in town the lights were orange and the snow was falling gold dust. I walked up Katie Roberts' stairs. I hesitated before I knocked, the snow falling down around me. I couldn't see a thing. There was no light anywhere. I knocked again. Spider opened the door.

Tess, he said softly. He didn't sound surprised.

A faint orange light came from the bedroom.

I said, Can I come in? and he opened the door wider.

Katie appeared, hugging her gold robe close around her body, the bed-spread robe she was wearing the day I first saw her. Her hair was tousled

and hung all loose around her shoulders. She smiled, so beautiful and damaged.

I said, I brought you Adam's letter. It's what you wanted, isn't it? It's
what you wanted all along?

Mama's Night of Dreams

She is on the roof of a tall building with Blue and Adam and Karen.
Far below, two highways cross, form an interchange, cut in four
directions through green and rolling countryside. The sun is going
down. The building is a skyscraper. It's time for them to leave. Inside, they're in a crowd. Everyone is leaving. Mama gets lost from
the others. People push around her, heading for the escalators.
Mama sees Adam and Karen and tries to follow them down. The
escalators are slides, and the one Mama's riding forks and divides.
She pitches herself to the left, still following, still sliding, and the
chute gets tubular and steep, almost vertical. She sees Blue ahead,
below her, backed into the polished wall, keeping himself from
moving until when she's in reach he lunges and closes his arms
around her. Hold on tight, he says, Don't let me lose you again,
and they slide down together, and the gravity begins to change.
They feel the pressure building around their bodies, coming at
them from all directions. Even sleeping, Mama feels it. She says
to Blue: The world could end before we get out of here. She says
this laughing, but the heaving scares her until they hit the bottom, standing on their feet. They are in a dark basement. They're

alone. Mama knows where they are. She's supposed to turn left. She doesn't want to go that way. But it leads to someplace she's supposed to be. She hesitates. A janitor looms up in front of her, big and shadowy, pushing a broom. She never sees his face, even though he lowers it close to hers. You can't go that way, he says, they're cleaning the bathrooms. He withdraws to the wall and a huge elevator door opens to reveal a suburban backyard, the yard of the house where Mama lived in L.A. when she was three and four and five, as if the door she and Blue have just stepped out through is the door of the room she always wanted for her own. To the right, on the lawn, they see two black cats and a family of kittens. The kittens are dressed in clothes. They are cooking and ironing and playing children's games. The two big cats are watching them, the way cats do. But the kittens aren't kittens. Out below their kitten fur, Mama sees little doll legs and rubber shoes. The kittens are puppets, dolls, the dolls Mama played with when she was a little girl, eight-inch little-girl dolls, Ginny dolls dressed up like kitten puppets dressed up like human beings. Mama doesn't like them. She turns away to the left, following Blue. A girl is there at a lemonade stand, selling bourbon. Blue takes one, on the rocks. The girl is eighteen or nineteen. She has dark curly hair and a pretty face. She's the kind of girl Blue always likes, but Mama isn't jealous. She asks the girl if she has plain lemonade, and the girl gets up and brings her a pitcher from under a wooden folding chair. Mama is very thirsty. Her thirst is so real it wakes her up, and she gets out of bed and drinks a glass of water.

She is going swimming. She walks along an L.A. sidewalk, carrying a towel. She is wearing her bathing suit, the blue-and-green plaid one she wore the summer she was thirteen. It has white trim and a short, pleated skirt. She is walking on the street where she lived then. She is going to the swimming pool. Suddenly she knows how silly she looks, because the bathing suit is silly. But I'm thin now, she thinks. I want to go. In the cement-block building, people in a short line move slowly toward the dressing rooms. Adam is sitting at a folding table to the left of the line. He looks up and smiles, and when she passes him, Mama ruffles his hair. He reaches back for her hand and holds on tight. But it is not her hand. It is the hand of someone behind her. Over her shoulder Mama says, You've got the wrong hand. She keeps on walking. She is happy, and for a while the dream is turquoise and smells of chlorine and sunshine and she knows nothing matters, he'll get the right hand again in time. But she can't wait for him there. She's on vacation with me and Grandma and China Blue. Tomorrow we have to leave, we are all going home. Mama is in the kitchen. We have just eaten dinner. Blue is resting in another room. Mama's clearing the table, scraping food off the plates, peppermint chicken in purple sauce. She puts all the parts away separately. She asks, Isn't anyone but me going to clean this mess up? and we don't answer and we don't help.

She is sleeping in Blue's bed, curled into his back. She dreams. She is crawling on his floor, her face approaching his sheets, Blue close behind her, pushing her up and onto the bed, almost in her, and the sight of those sheets—filthy with menstrual blood, lost earrings, tufts of hair—those sheets so close to her eyes knock her out. She loses whole minutes, goes under, until Blue, in her dream within a dream, touches her shoulder from behind and pulls her up from emptiness, frightened, offering consolation. She wakes up and feels his shoulder under her cheek. He rolls toward her and his face divides, one half his, the other chunks of uncooked meat.

She is on a New York subway platform. She wants the train for L.A. She is waiting on the wrong level. She sees the train below her. She goes deeper down. The train is so narrow she rides it standing. The longer she rides, the narrower it gets, narrower than a coffin. She is riding sideways, looking out a window with nothing beyond it. The train gets smaller and smaller, until Mama is bigger than it is. She is standing on a dune. The tracks disappear downward, as if buried into the sand. There are no tracks, only ruts where they ran. The dune is narrow, a high ridge. Mama stands alone there, under a bright sun, surrounded by water, far away.

She lives on a farm with Florida Carter. A beggar woman comes to the door, withered and shabby and dirty and old. She puts out her hand, asking for money or food. Her fingers are callused. She won't go away. Florida stabs her. Mama watches the knife go in. They go on about their chores. They are very busy, scrubbing out big cooking pots. All the time Mama talks, says it wasn't her fault, it was only her idea, she didn't think Florida really meant to do it, and Florida just smiles, her Cheshire Catlike Florida smile, until some man comes knocking, asking for the old woman. Mama never sees him. Florida sends him away. Mama and Florida are in the barn, digging in the straw. They uncover yellow bones. Mama's standing by the river, holding her right eye in her left hand. She's carried it around like that for a long time. She opens her hand. The eye is dry and shriveled, a little green grape with a red spot on it, soft and decaying. If she throws it into the river, no one will know her part in killing the old woman. Mama's eye is the evidence against her. She thinks the old woman must have been her mother—my grandma, who is alive and lives alone in Oregon, where we sometimes go to see her. The water is black. Mama looks at the eye in her hand. She throws it and watches it fall. When it hits the water, she wakes up. She thinks the dream is real. She tries to open her eyes. They won't open. She reaches for her face. She feels her eye in its socket. Her cold fingers wake her again. Her room is dark, but light slips in the alley window off the street. She sees the outlines of the woodwork, the dresser, the reading lamp, the chair.

She is riding a train, the European kind with compartments where strangers face one another. She is in her compartment alone. Her bags are on the seat with her. The train comes into a station. She wants to go to the bathroom. She has to get off the train. She leaves her bags where they are. She leaves her purse. When she comes back, the train is gone. On other tracks, there are other trains. She speaks to a conductor. She doesn't know how to explain. She doesn't know how to get her things back or how to catch up with them. Her ticket is on the train. She doesn't know how to choose another train that will be the right one. She doesn't know where that train was going. She only knows she has to reach its destination.

I am leading her through a house where I've been hired to cut an old man's hair. I've brought her with me to show her the house because it is so strange. She follows me through high granite rooms with curving, windowless walls. When we round a turn into a long space filled with light, she sees the old man, propped up against his pillows, wearing a nightshirt, his hair long and white, and a short woman, his wife, his nurse, standing beside him. I tell her I've brought Mama, and the woman is surprised, but pleased. She brings me a bowl of water and scissors and a liquid, lemony-smelling soap, and takes Mama down the other end of the long, open room. They stop at a couch and glass table, where she offers Mama wine and talks about the years she spent in Provincetown with the old man. Now they come up for summers, she says. She wants to show Mama her recipe books. She wants to show her the pictures of her children. She leads Mama into the kitchen, an alcove at the end of the long room. They are turning the pages of the album of photographs and recipes when Mama looks up and out the window sees a crowd of short round women pushing toward the door, women who remind her of Florida Carter, they have her big mouth, her big dark eyes. But these women are shorter and round. They have flatter faces, black hair instead of hennaed brown. They are third-world women, women from some hungry, damaged, war-torn place, and when Mama looks back at her hostess she understands that the women outside are the woman's daughters. You must both stay to dinner, the woman says. That would be nice, Mama says. She is drinking her wine. The woman says how happy she is I brought Mama along, it's more fun to have two, and the daughters pour in the kitchen door, surrounding Mama, pressing against her. They are all very glad she has come, very glad she is staying. They crush her in their delight. They smile, they never stop smiling, and one of them pinches Mama's forearm, pulling at her flesh, saying, Yes, she'll do, and lets it fall back to the bone. Mama understands. They mean to eat her. They mean to eat me. She struggles her way through their bodies, shouting my name. She has to warn me. Tess, she cries, running back up the long room. She is afraid she is too late, running nowhere while the room gets longer, crying, Tess, Tess, so frightened she wakes herself with her silent screams.

She lives with Florida Carter in a loft in New York. She is sitting at their kitchen table talking to a visitor, a matronly woman with a flowered dress and blue hair. In the dream, Florida is a painter, and the woman has come to look at her paintings. On the other side of the sheetrock wall, Florida is tidying up. She appears around the partition. She says, Ready. She leads the woman into the studio, Mama following. She says, Sorry about the mess, it's hard to keep a place clean when all you have is a mattress. She sweeps her hand toward the floor. It is dark in the studio. The paintings are pale and small. Mama thinks the woman won't like them, because they are not beautiful. She thinks she won't like them either, but for other reasons. She stops following. She wanders away. She goes downstairs, goes outside. The night is full of mosquitoes, foggy and lit with orange lights. She is walking with a woman named André who is wearing a black coat and looks like Grace Kelly in *The Country Girl*. Mama's skin is covered with bug spray. She feels sick from it, but also thinks she hasn't used enough. She goes to a corner stand selling plastic party cups filled with a clear, apricot-colored liquid that repels mosquitoes when you drink it. She buys a cup. At the first sip, she feels faint. No, she says. No, there's something wrong.

Her body shivers. Nausea blacks out the night. She collapses to the sidewalk. People crowd around her. André is behind her, bending over. She grabs Mama's shoulders. Mama feels herself shudder. André is all she knows: her hands on her shoulders, her voice addressing the crowd: *She's having convulsions*. But suddenly Mama says, No, and shakes off André's hands, crying, Blue, I want Blue, not *that* Blue, *my* Blue. Blue, she screams, Blue, Blue, and wakes herself up. Her skin is cold and sticky. Her mouth tastes of poison, chemicals, insect repellent. She gets up and goes to the kitchen and drinks half a bottle of grapefruit juice, looking out the narrow window at the beach. Gray light rises vaguely into the sky.

She is at a party. It is her mother's house in Oregon but not her mother's house; this is a house much bigger, but the atmosphere is the same, everything glass and cedar and pine. All the rooms are crowded. None of the people is anyone real. A young woman is with her. Maybe it's Florida Carter, maybe it's Karen, maybe it's André, maybe it's me. It's no one in particular, just a young woman, someone Mama's hanging out with, another stranger at this party full of strangers. They wander from room to room. They giggle together, like schoolgirls. They ogle the men, the boys. They are standing on a deck, in a small circle of people, everyone talking and drinking, when Mama's father looms up in front of her, climbing up over the rail. His skin is yellow, peeling and blotchy. She stops her conversation. She says, Are you dead? Aren't you dead yet? she says, Daddy, you're dead, and he grins at her and answers, Yes, I'm dead, and slowly fades away. She stares at the place where he stood. Other people stand there now, closing the circle. She turns to the people on her left and her right. She says, Did you see him? Didn't you see me talking to my father? and they tell her they saw her talking but no one was there. Then a voice, from her right, behind her, says: I saw him, and Mama looks around, expecting to see Adam. She feels thankful. She isn't crazy. She did see a ghost. Or a kind of ghost. She wasn't the only one to see him. But Adam isn't there, only the crowd of strangers and the woman-girl, who might be Florida, or Karen, or André, or me.

A man, dying of some disease, gasping for breath, is in Mama's care. He's an old friend, a man she went to college with and lost track of years ago. But he is not her old friend. She knows the man is not her old friend but not who he is. He is gasping for breath. Mama can help him by going to him, pulling him up so he's sitting, something very simple. She doesn't do it and he dies. She knows she killed him. She had no reason to. She stood there bewitched while he gasped for breath, and she didn't move. She stood there and watched him die. She and Blue are packing up their things. It's an office they're closing. They are in L.A. The dead man is on the couch, still in his bed sheets, his mouth gaping open. Blue is sitting at a desk, going through some papers. Mama is pacing. The man is dead. She and Blue killed him. She killed him. Blue killed him. The man is dead. They have to get rid of the body. The scene never changes. Blue sits at the desk, going through the papers, his, Mama's, the dead man's—Mama never knows. She paces, worrying about the body, seeing the man's face dying, begging for breath. She tells herself she didn't kill him, the disease killed him, or maybe Blue tells her that. She doesn't believe it. If she didn't kill him, why do they have to hide the body, why do they have to run? And, still, here they are. Not hiding the body.

Not running. The scene doesn't change. Blue sits at the desk, going through the papers, and Mama paces, watching the dead man die. Slowly, the repetition wakes her. She lies there in the gray dark, listening to the room. She understands. She doesn't know how. It just comes to her. Suddenly. She is cold. She gets up, grabbing her glasses, her robe, still half-naked leaves her room. Sunrise blinds her. The water and sky are pink and silver. She bangs her knee against a chair in her hurry to get to me. She stops at my door. She already knows what she'll find there. She's quiet. She turns my doorknob slowly. She pushes. She hopes she'll hear my steady breathing. She doesn't hear it. She pushes the door open. My bed is empty. I have gone.

Winterkill

He wakes up to a terrible smell, the smell of fear. Nothing but fear
pouring out his body could smell so sharp and sour, so full of
death and decay. In the room something is beautiful. I. He. You.
China Blue is going home. Every voice the mind. You are looking at something beautiful and smelling that terrible smell. It is
light reflecting silver off the wood grain of a chair. Home to be
erased. You will be sorry to leave this room. Last night he started
packing. Not just for summer. For good. Boxes are spread around
the floor, clothes in piles, towels, sheets, brown plastic trash bags—
his laundry, things to throw away, things to keep. When he came
in, an image caught his eye. It made you want to draw. It was
only his white Irish sweater, bunched up over the back of a chair,
reflected into the night. I drew it dreaming. It floated, white in
the darkness, an academic study, finely rendered in graphite or
charcoal, unidentifiable, pure form. He reaches down to the floor
and gropes for his cigarettes. His curtains are open. Pale pink light
fills the room. He can't have slept five hours. He was up half the
night, rummaging, sorting, folding, stacking, kicking, loading, stiff
and without words complaining to the dust and cardboard, the
snow, the glass, the walls.

He finds a cigarette but no matches. He hesitates before rising, lets himself fall back to his sheets. Get up. Get moving. Open the doors, get rid of the smell, pack, keep packing. The room is warm, the heat set high. He breaks the cigarette with his thumb against his fingers and drops it to the floor, falls back and sits again, hugging his knees. Across the room on the white plastic table next to a bottle of dead flowers a peanut butter jar holds pencils, ballpoints, an aqua blue non-repro pen from his job at the Advocate, an exacto knife, pushpins, thumbtacks, crayons, and a half-used matchbook. He leans against the cold wall. I have a bottle of flowers, left over from October, the water evaporated, the bottle clouded with the residue of slime. Once it held grapefruit juice. We drank it when Holly had the flu. The flowers came from Tess. She brought them here for brunch one day. I was having a party. I—a person with no name, a person with a history that if it ended this morning couldn't fill a postcard: Born. Left home. Hid. Died.

Holly, a gray shadow in the fogged glass, walks up your driveway, an absence, a wish, a ghost.

He gets out of bed, pulls on his jeans, crosses the room. He flips on the television. He boils water. He makes coffee. He changes the channels, looking for cartoons. He lights a cigarette and sits down on the edge of the bed. That stranger wrote to her. Another man in hiding, another man running from a history he forgets. I've hid out here too long. I don't know how to begin. I'm only thirty. And it's as if I'm already dead.

You remember the smell.

He picks his shirt up off the floor and half puts it on, letting it hang unbuttoned while he slides the glass door open. The morning is brittle. Gooseflesh rises on your chest, down your arms. You stand looking over the treetops, the housetops, down to the water. Everything is breakable, white, brown, blue. Etched in crystal. The morning is ringing. The cold reaches into your balls, your anus, the chill climbs your spine. He closes the door. The glass sweats. On the television Tom and Jerry race a speedboat on a lake, fishing for a trumpet-playing trout that runs on tail fins over the surface of the water. The smell is still in the room. The smell is on your body, in your sheets. He strips the bed and bundles the linens into the laundry bag. He folds the blankets and piles them up. He puts the pillows on top. He sits on the bare, green-striped mattress and smokes another cigarette. A teenager, blond ponytail bobbing, sprawls upside down on a couch, giggling into the telephone. A baby crawls out of the house. Tom, holding Jerry in his paw, releases him and runs to rescue the baby. When he settles it back in its carriage, the girl, crying Bad cat, bad cat, beats Tom with a broom.

Take a shower, wash this stink off.

Blithely, the baby continues its travels, carried away in a dump truck, riding a construction elevator high over the city, making its way from bare steel beam to bare steel beam, followed and saved again and again by Tom, by Jerry, crawling on unconscious and unscathed.

He stands under scalding water, soaping his armpits, his neck, his hairless chest. I have the body of an adolescent boy, long and meatless, muscles that never filled, all cock and feet and fingers and balls. I am stronger than I look. I am larger than my body. Thirty. Going home to mother for the first time in seven years. Or maybe not. I wash behind my ears, between my toes. I am a good boy. See, Mommy?—clean. He wraps his hips in a heavy towel.

He shaves. He splashes himself with Chanel for Men. He puts on a white shirt, his newest pair of jeans. The room is white now. The sky is white. He opens the north door, facing the driveway. The sun is breaking through slowly. A thaw is coming. Thin snow covers the ground. Holly, bundled against the cold, walks up the frozen sand. He leaves the door open and goes back to the bed to wait. The Pink Panther's fairy godmother gives him a pair of roller skates that crash him into a pane of glass, down bowling alley lanes, through a car wash, and dead-end him reeling against a brick wall. He can't get the skates off his feet, can't stop skating. They pull him onto a tennis court and slam him into the net, the net hurls him flying to the zoo, a gorilla punches him up in the air again, and an elephant, catching him with his trunk, flips him over and pounds his head into the ground.

Holly finds him packing and watching cartoons.

I knew you'd come, he says.

It was summer when he met her, after Labor Day, the crowds gone and the days still long, the afternoons saturated with gold shadows and heat. All over town, restaurant workers were having end-of-season parties. She was sitting in the Fo'c'sle, at a table full of friends. Sun slanted in the glass and edged her hair, her hands, her bright green long-neck Rolling Rock bottle. She laughed and her voice was quick, her mind flashing out her eyes. Her blouse was blue, cool against her sun-flushed skin. Her silver earrings gleamed. They barely said ten words to each other: where they worked, whether the work continued. His didn't, hers did. How long he'd been around. How long had she? It was another month before he spoke to her again. She asked what he used to do then, where he came from, where he was going. He didn't know.

Nowhere, he said, what about you? and she forgot her question and answered his. She used to work in New York. A news job. It was a good job. She laughed. She'd given it up. She didn't like what it meant, she said. It wasn't worth the price. She had a daughter, almost thirteen. She was older than he'd thought she was. Thirty-four. And he not thirty yet, not then. She didn't have plans. She was waiting. She didn't know. He either. Everybody in this town could be doing something else.

She's standing in the open doorway.

Tess is missing, she says.

She comes in. She slides the glass door closed behind her.

In summer he moved away from this place, to a room in the center of town, big enough for a bed, his boxes, a motel refrigerator, a hot plate, some nails. Only the windows made it bearable, three long narrow panes of glass, with screens, facing morning, the water, the street. Last summer, for three or four days at a time, she lived with him in that room, until he sent her away. In summer there were other women, always other women. Occasions for her jealousy. He was in love with maybe seven that summer. In love, he said. Sometimes he wanted to fuck them. Twice he even asked. Mostly he wrote them off as out of reach. They trusted him, they turned to him, they cried on his shoulder. You saw yourself as safe, and so did they. Only Holly saw you differently. Not safe, she said. She was laughing: You can remember me forever as the one who knew you weren't safe. He was faithful to her in spite of himself. In summer they talked about love. In summer she said, I think any woman who says no to you is crazy, and he laughed and answered, So do I. In summer she told him about Adam. In summer they watched that fire from his windows and saw Katie Roberts and

Adam out in the street together and didn't go down. In summer, she taught you to remember. In summer, she unsettled you. In summer, Tess was gone. To Tucson, to her father. Tess has a father, and it isn't you. When did Holly become so necessary to me? This tarbaby relationship, he finally said. Every move I make to free myself pulls me deeper in.

She slides the glass door closed behind her. The past is here now. She is still arriving. Arriving forever. You feel yourself withdrawing from something. The light turns acid, corrosive. The sun is rising in the white cold sky. The wind is blowing. For a month last year I hid in this room. John Hinckley tried to kill the president and when I hit the streets I bought a gun. You didn't buy bullets. You kept it under the bed. He wanted to be part of a statistic. That gun exists to be used. Without bullets, a gun is not a gun. Chekhov's rule is a rule of reality, not literature—counting up the big guns on the planet aimed mostly at each other, counting up the little guns in jungles, forests, deserts, cities, huts, shacks, tents, armories, basements, apartments, houses, caves. From Vietnam his brother had written, *Flying bullets snap when they pass over your head. You hear them go snapping.* I thought of insects. Snap, snap. I stared at my clipping of Alexander Haig. I met Adam and didn't like him. You wanted to protect her. It wasn't Adam you didn't like, but what he could do to her. The same thing you could do. In summer, you saw that sickness in her that could love only the maimed. In summer, she scared you, the way she scared you last winter, walking up your hill. Then summer ended. She changed. Tess came home. He moved back into his hermit house and stopped trying to leave her. She made you feel your emptiness. She made you know your own diseases. You envied her clarity and hid from it.

You envied her capacity to step outside herself and let you go. She never let me go. It wasn't real. It was an act. You needed her and hated needing. When Adam showed up in town again, I sat in this room and held my gun and told myself I knew this story: With this gun you are meant to kill the stranger. You are meant to be the stranger and unwittingly to kill him. He is your father, your father lost at sea. But you can make your own journey, you can leave them all behind, you can go back into the world. It is never too late to go back into the world. That was what Adam's coming meant. The story goes on and on. I sat here with that gun I bought the day China Blue tore through the paper sky and I did not want the daughter and I did not want the mother. You did not want anything. There was no one you wanted to kill, no one you wanted to save. You wanted everything to die. You wanted everything to live but you. You were tired of your mind, not even your body. This body can survive, you said, what do I care? and when Adam left without seeing her, you put your empty gun back under this bed.

I suppose you said something to her, he says when she's finally in the room. You should have talked to me last night, not to her.

Don't tell me what I should have done. Tess is missing I said.

One night she shrieked at him and after he left her, he heard nothing but her shrieking. More often she withdrew, saw him with a pretty woman, flashed eyes, something coiling cold up into her. Later she complained, to him in terror, to friends in tears. Later still, she understood. He had no privacy, no secrets, not even secrets he withheld, secrets he hardly knew he had to hide until he heard them back from her—or roundabout, from someone else from someone else from someone who heard them from her. It was a fat letter, that letter she had from Adam.

And you think I have her hidden here, is that it? You think I'm getting ready to spirit her away?

What he remembers of his other women is the cities they existed in: one in Chicago, one in San Francisco, one in New York. The isolated moments. Blowing the wisp of brown hair away from her lips where it fell while she held the phone with a shoulder and used her hands to open the mail. Laughing when the downpour came suddenly, the sun making rainbows while the water thinned her white blouse, showing skin, the tight little nipples unprotected by the chains and coins and rings of brass hanging from her neck. Fishing in her oversized tapestry bag for the subway token she never had until in his impatience he dug in his pocket and went to the booth, all the while conscious of those skinny black-stockinged legs, those bones, that angle of helplessness below the knees. He loved the moments. Only the moments, never the women. And Holly, in October, the afternoon light coming in on her hair: But did you love them? And he: I loved them the way I love you. And she: But were never in love? And he: Once, but it was an illusion. She: But you want to be in love? Something's missing without it? And he: Yes. And she: But have never been in love with the women you've lived with, the women you've actually known? In your life? And he: No. And she, after a silence, sitting here at the white plastic table when the flowers were fresh, wearing faded blue jeans and that blue cotton shirt, smoking Marlboros and letting her hair grow again slowly, shaking her head, in and out of the sun, she: As if you can't love a woman who's real, but only one who's absent, in your imagination? Then I'm sorry for you and sorry for any woman who thinks she loves you.

You knew she was right. I knew she was wrong. He had never seen her so clearly as in that moment. She was talking about herself. But before he could answer she stood up and picked up her jacket and walked out and walked away. You loved a woman who didn't exist. A woman between the mother and the daughter. As if you had been the daughter's father, years ago. You loved them both and neither. He didn't know how it happened. Not at the beginning. Not at the end. Nowhere in between. Somehow. Always. Until he was standing at the bar in the Governor Bradford telling Katie Roberts: Holly got a letter from Adam today. And Katie, as if she cared less, hidden in her heavy-lidded eyes: Any news? And he: I don't know, she didn't open it while I was there. And twenty-four hours later, that kid, her lover, Spider: This man fucked your daughter. And Holly here in front of him, standing in his room while he packs, going nowhere, going home. *How?* you want to ask. *What?* you want to scream. *Tess is missing?*

You want to cry. Far away from yourself, you know you want to cry.

Are you going somewhere? she's asking.

Holly, Holly. He stares at her. Holly. Stop me. Look around.

That gesture she made, back before the beginning, when he took her home falling down from too much wine at Thanksgiving and she said did he want to stay. Not tonight, he answered, confused, maybe another time, but asked to kiss her, and she flung up her arms—the right shielding her face, the left extended, warding him off, together forming a cross—unconscious, warding off devils, warding off blows. A gesture so rich he stood there stunned. A gesture she repeated two months later, that first January, an hour before she cut off her hair. He was trying to leave her. You sat there at that table saying no to her, No, no. I'm going now, I said, I'm leaving, let me kiss you goodbye, and up came those hands. A gesture so primitive you had to call her attention to it. You made that gesture at Thanksgiving, he said. It fascinated me. But she didn't remember. She had no memory of how Thanksgiving ended at all. In the morning she had to call someone to find out how she got home.

What's this? she asked in the half-dark three weeks later, reading his boxed letters through the plexiglass, and he squeezed her neck, she turned and he kissed her. I can't stay, she said, yielding, Tess is home. Come with me, she said, and he went. From the first moment I saw you, he said, I knew we'd end up in bed. She laughed against his skinny chest. She said, I know. I've been lusting after you. Lusting? he repeated. Well, maybe not lusting, she said, lusting is too impersonal. I've been wanting you, she said. Me in particular? He thought it was funny. But she meant it, and she frightened him, and already you began to run. You saw your mother tying your shoes. You saw your mother the night your father's boat didn't come in, her body already folding into age, your sister chattering, distracting her, serving peas, frozen peas, overcooked. You remember those peas, your mother nodding, listening, growing smaller inside the wind and the rain, the hands you saw then for the first time old, the knuckles, the bones exactly like yours, in withered skin, and you, thirteen and your brother in boot camp, suddenly the man of the house. You wouldn't believe it. You looked at your mother's blue veins, her trembling flesh.

What is this? Holly asked again a month later, your third night, the first you spent together in this room. Someone I used to know, he said. What happened to him? she asked, and you told her he gave up art, he works on Wall Street now. But he finally got his paintings back? she asked. They were damaged, you told her. Deliberately destroyed. Couldn't he sue? she asked. Who knows? you said, he didn't do it. He just gave up? she asked, and you didn't answer. Was he any good? she wanted to know. What does it matter? you said. He quit. How could he have been good? She was looking at you funny. She was reading your mind. You shivered. Come on, he said. It's an old story. Let's go to bed.

Home to mother, he tells her. Isn't that what you think I should do? Isn't that what you've thought I should do all along?

If she reached out her hand and let that glassy calm leave her face, she would know I'm angry. She made you remember everything. A childhood in which your mother tied your shoes till you were eight years old. A childhood in which your mother would have tied your shoes forever if from shame you hadn't made her stop. A brother dead in a jungle more remote than the moon. A sister married pregnant at nineteen home childless at twenty. A father so hidden and taciturn his final absence could have gone almost unnoticed if you hadn't feared the meaning of the vagueness of his death. The letters boxed in plastic, the other women, the false names, the cities, the lies. The look on her face when that boy accused you, that shock of believing, that stillness of unsurprise. I would like to shake her. If I could put my hands on her arms I would break that calm, she would scream, scratch, cry, rest her head against my shoulder, let me stroke her hair, sob and catching her breath begin to listen to what I say. But I can't touch her. The poison in your mouth prevents you, the ice in your body, the smell in the room.

But like this? she says. All of a sudden?

Her words echo. On the television, a bulldog, cat-clawed into a grid like a ham about to be baked, falls apart and reassembles. She believes I fucked her daughter. A boy, almost a stranger, spoke to her in a bar and she stared at me, saying nothing, and saying nothing to me now, thinks I did it, looks around my half-stripped room and thinks I'm packing up because I did it, thinks I'm leaving, all of a sudden, because I did it, because you did, because Tess is missing, thinks Tess is missing because I did. As if it were possible.

Are you going to believe everything you hear on the street?

Her eyes stop wandering. She wants to believe I'm guilty. I am not guilty. I am not. She wants to believe it. If China Blue is guilty, she is innocent. We are two wind-up toys. We move in our spring-tight paces, collide with obstacles, each other, our plastic feet whirring, our gears grinding, slowly winding down. This woman loved me and denied it. She thought I loved her like a mother, for telling stories with, for keeping warm through the night. Words wound the body, she said once. Words made us what we are.

Her eyes stop wandering. She says, I want to know the truth.

The sun is strong now, the light. If the thaw comes too quickly, the whole town will go crazy. Holly's hair is hanging in her eyes. She brushes it away and it falls again. She is waiting for the truth. He doesn't know what the truth is. You've forgotten. Maybe I never knew. He listened to their voices in the mornings, waiting in her bed. He listened to the sounds of breakfast and orange juice, the sounds of leaving for work and school. He listened to Tess laughing. She was a child. Not quite a little girl. But there was another Tess. The Tess of the off-moment. You caught her look in the rear-view mirror when they rode in your car, you saw it alone with her when she talked, you saw it when she sat in corners watching—the Tess who is not her mother, not the Tess of her father either, the secret Tess, the Tess herself, the Tess who makes you wonder what this girl really is: the missing Tess, the Tess who is missing.

I love her, Holly. You made her beautiful.

The room is full of white sky and wind. We sat around drinking coffee on Sundays, reading the Times. I looked at the ads in the magazine and made remarks about the women, the objects in the photos, the Steuben glass, the fresh-cut roses on mahogany tables, the rugs from Einstein Moomjy, the underwear, the jewelry, the furs. I said maybe I should go back to the modern world and get myself a real job. So you can buy things? Holly said. What's wrong with things? I said. Tess laughed. Mama has no respect for things, she said. What happened to the future? Holly said once. When did they take it away? The future is now, I told her. There never has been a future. No one can touch it. Holly said, Tell Alexander Haig, and Tess made a face. Come off it, Mama, she said, and Holly laughed and grabbed an orange from the bowl on the table and threw it to her and didn't know what to say. Tess and I did the crossword, and sometimes I went home, and sometimes I stayed. The days got shorter. We ate Christmas dinner. Holly cooked a duck. Jane came and drank champagne. The girls got silly and we laughed with them. They told us stories from school.

She's missing, Holly says.

There must be a villain and there must be a clown, a fool. I would prefer to be the fool. I keep dead flowers and dreams. I protect myself and children. I rave at kings and princes in words they will not understand. I shout nonsense to the rooftops, and only the innocent laugh, and the birds. My innocence is my wickedness. I go dancing on the graves. Missing? I want to say. My father missing at sea, my sister missing in her mind, my brother missing in action until what might have been his body came back in a sealed box. She wants to talk to me about missing? She touched her father's body, she held his cold head between her hands. What does she know about missing? I've been missing for seven years. I go on living. The missing never die.

She's missing, Holly says again.

So go look for her, Holly.

He walks past her to the door and slides it open: Get the fuck out of here and go look for her.

He leans his head against the glass. Her bootsteps come quietly on the slate behind him. She hesitates. He turns before she can touch him, staring, his face as withdrawn as hers has been. You are going home after seven years because this woman who made you remember, who won't say she loves you, who's known you better than you've ever known yourself, believes you fucked her daughter, and even though it can't be, you know it must be true. You watch her leave, step by step down the red bricks gleaming through the snow, passing the car, half-loaded with boxes, down the driveway on the ice and sand, turning up into the trees. She is gone. The room is cold now. From the television Bugs Bunny says, *Hello, Earth*, then stops himself to ask, *If that's the Earth, then where the cotton pickin' heck am I?* You can't escape the smell. He goes back to the bed. Bugs is dangling in the fist of Hugo the Abominable Snowman, a white King Kong. Holly is gone. Tess is gone. Bugs steals a flying saucer and the Snowman frisbees him to Earth. He lies back and closes his eyes. *That's all folks.* Every story is the same. In the world of cartoons, every character is a loner, only adversary relationships survive. There are no families. The Disney hero is an orphan. Lovers never marry, except after a magical rescue from a magical death, at the end of a story that ends. Show me a reality that ever ends. Show me a family. Show me a hero who talks to anyone but himself. Show me the value of a single event, the truth of anything happening.

Holly.

Over Road Runner's beeps, he cries her name to the room. Holly—bolting up from the bed, to the door, down the wet snowy stairs barefoot, two at a time, running the slope to the bottom of the driveway, calling *Holly*, but she's too far gone and out of sight, he's standing on the frozen sand, calling her name, feeling the thaw on the tops of his feet, the cold sun on his skin, panting and watching his breath cloud, his tears ice in the wind.

Secrets

Climbing the frozen sand, Mama heard Blue call her name and kept on walking. Hearing her name on the cold air behind her, she thought of Eurydice, who went to hell and chose to stay there—an unorthodox interpretation, she said once to Florida Carter, but probably true. It was a beautiful morning, the clouds white and breaking, the sun glistening off the wet melting snow. To become willing to be guilty, to become willing to cause pain, to become soiled, willing to face the other's pain, to acknowledge causing it: she walked home with thoughts like these. (Why am I alone, Blue? she'd asked him once. She had felt like screaming it. What? he said. You're alone because you want to be. Don't you know that yet? They were riding in the car. She didn't remember speaking.) At the door the cat meowed and rubbed against her legs. She didn't have to look to see I wasn't back. She looked anyway. My bed was still empty. She sat down at the table. Not true, she told herself. This cannot be true. Tess, she said aloud. She stood up and went outside and walked down the deck stairs to the beach, shading her eyes. Tess, she called. She looked in both directions for a figure that might have been mine. She walked the beach, calling my name. The air was cold and salty. The sand where she walked was wet, the tide going out, the moisture seeping into her thin leather boots. Her hair blew around her face. Seagulls hovered close to the water and dove and swooped away. She called my name and searched the shadows under landings, between pilings. She walked fast, as if she had a destination. At the breakwater she stopped. The wind cut into her cheeks. The sky went white, blue. She looked at the black, ragged line of rock spanning the harbor to Long Point and believed in her body that she knew where I was. *I know*, she thought and climbed the rocks and listened for her body to tell her. Squinting, she searched the line of sand across the water. She waited. The water plashed against the rocks. Seagulls cried. She climbed down again and turned back the way she came.

She ran. Thinking *I know, I don't know, I know.* Wanting words to fill the empty knowing in the hollow below her ribs—that part of her body that had always stayed thin, except when she was pregnant with me, and even then absorbed me into her somehow so that the short smock dresses she wore, a style in 1967, were enough to conceal her condition and riding the crowded bus to her job in San Francisco while my father went to Oakland to demonstrate against the draft, she had to thrust her hips deliberately forward if she wanted the young men in business suits reading *The Wall Street Journal* to realize they were sitting while a pregnant woman stood. In New York, she said years later, someone would have given me a seat. She ran. Wanting words to rise up out of her body and tell her where I was. I'm not afraid of anything, she'd said to Adam and the words were flesh and she knew them only when they came laughing out of her mouth, *I'm not afraid of anything, I am in love with you and I have been for a real long time,* and for something like twenty-four hours they believed it and believed each other. Until Blue phoned wanting to take her for a ride. Adam asked could he wait alone there till it was time to go to the airport—Karen was flying in for the weekend—and when Blue came they shook hands. Then Mama turned away to follow him out and Adam stopped her saying, Just remember, you left first—as if two hours later he wasn't leaving himself to pick up Karen, as if the next week he wouldn't be fucking Florida Carter and two weeks after that wouldn't leave them all for Katie Roberts. As if that detail, Mama leaving, breaking the spell, was the omen he'd been watching for. As if everything could be that simple.

Mama ran. The salt air and wind made tears. On the beach below our deck she saw Mason walking his dog. He was bundled in brown and gray, his hands shoved deep in his pockets, his shoulders hunched. The arthritic black retriever, planted stiff-legged in the sand, barked at three fat seagulls standing motionless at the waterline. Mama slowed down and wiped her eyes. Mason, she called. He looked up. Have you seen Tess this morning? Have you seen Tess anywhere?

Mason blinked. Tess is missing? he said.

I don't know, Mama said. I'm not sure. Come in when Banner's done. I want to talk to you.

She took off her coat. She opened a can of food for the cat. She started a pot of coffee. She sat at the table and lit a cigarette, unpleasantly conscious of the smell of her own body. She pulled off her boots. She got the phone and dialed Jane's.

She's still asleep, her father said.

I'm looking for Tess, Mama said.

What did she do, stay out all night?

Mason appeared in the window, urging Banner up the deck stairs. Mama gestured for them to come in.

It's this morning, she said to Jane's father. A few hours . . . I don't know.

Relax, he said. She's the most responsible kid in town.

There's more to it, Mama said. I need to talk to Jane.

One more call, she said to Mason while Banner laid himself out at her feet. Get yourself some coffee.

But at Rainy's no one was home.

If you're really worried, Mason said, you should call the police.

What would I call the police for?

They can find her for you. Nothing has to be wrong. This is a little town.

Something is wrong, Mason, she said. Sit down.

But she couldn't tell him. She went abstract. She lit a cigarette and looked out the window at the water.

Fascination is interior, she said. Fascination happens at a distance from the occasion that incites it. But knowledge doesn't come through the eyes. Sometime or other, you have to choose. You have to give up fascination. You have to know that what's real is more important than you are, and that looking isn't enough, that looking at anything all you see is what you take there, that to see more than you start with you have to move in so close you can't see it anymore, you have to stop looking at things believing you can see them whole because you can't look at things whole and the only thing you explore when you look at things whole is yourself, your own process of seeing, never what's there. What's there is specific,

124

she said. And what's specific is never whole. That's all. You have to abandon fascination if you want to live in what's real. It's a choice you have to make, she said. I always thought I chose for the truth, she said. But the truth I chose for was the cleanness of myself, keeping my hands clean, keeping my nose clean. I mean—do you know what I mean? she asked, turning back to him. I thought I was after what was real but what's real is what I've always run from. Because what's real is beyond me. It's always beyond, out of reach. It doesn't lend itself to truth, or to knowledge, or to cleanness. It doesn't yield. It's insistent. Just there. Fascinating. But as fascination it keeps you at a distance. You have to break the fascination of yourself to get to it, to get inside. I thought that's what I was doing with Blue, she said. But I was wrong. And now ...

Now *what*, Holly? Mason asked. What is it?

Now something's happened, she said. I can't tell you. I thought I could tell you.

Is he running out on you again? Is that it?

Tess is missing, she said.

Mason sighed. He said, If you think it's serious, you really should call the police.

People like me don't call the police, Mama said.

What do you want me to do, Holly?

She closed her eyes. She thought that with her eyes closed she might be able to tell him. Blue—, she began. She shook her head. There's a kid in town who told me—, she said. *In the bar. Last night. With that woman.* She opened her eyes. Last night, she said. I have to talk to that boy. He'll know something.

She asked Mason to wait there. In case I came home. In case Jane called back.

125

Tell her to get over here, Mama said. Tell her to find Rainy if she can and get herself over here. See if she sounds like she understands.

Sure, Mason said. He smiled. He said, Bring me a *Times*.

She walked the slushy street, half her mind remembering, half breaking darkness into logical propositions, sorting chaos into lists. She walked looking—into uncurtained windows, up alleys, over fences, down at the beach. She walked—walking out every panic she'd ever walked out on that street. She'd walked it the winter before, that night in January, barefoot in the snow. She walked it the next morning, to work, with her sudden short hair, at the restaurant asking no one in particular, Where's Adam Pearson with his big bottle of vodka? She walked it in the night to Blue in a gale. She walked it last spring, that April Sunday, sharing secrets with Florida Carter and hoping to be seen. She walked it four days later, shattered, all the way to the Truro line. That street was in her body. Her life was in that street. She walked it thinking: This street knows more than I do. This street knows where Tess is. Thinking: *Blue. Your friend.* And Tess understood. And now she's gone. Because she didn't want to tell me. Blue's going home to his mother and Tess is gone. Because it's true? Or because it might be true? Or because I showed them both I could believe it might be true? Because it isn't? Or because it is? Where did it come from if it isn't true? That boy? But if he heard it from Tess (and what else can he tell me?—*because Tess understood the question*), nothing changes. Either it's a lie and she ran from the lie or it's the truth and she ran from the truth. Or something in between. Mama shivered. The day was getting warmer. Melting snow ran in the gutters. Shovels scraped on the sidewalks. Her eyes watered. She wanted her sunglasses. The day was bright. She walked in the sand-covered street and moved aside for cars. Have you seen Tess? she asked anyone she knew. The meat rack was empty, the benches gleaming. Have you seen that boy? she asked in the restaurant. That boy that hangs out on the meat rack, she said, that friend of Tess and Rainy and Jane's? Spider, someone said from the kitchen. But no one had seen him. Where does he live? Mama asked. Does anyone know where he lives?

The stairwell was dark. Mama knocked at Spider's door. She waited and knocked again. She tried the door and pushed it in. She stopped just over the threshold, the door standing open, her hand still on the knob—she thought Spider might come home. The room was big and bright and undivided. She cataloged its contents: a refrigerator, a hot plate, a sink, a kerosene heater, a raised cement shower with a mildewed pink plastic curtain, a sawed-off piece of log he must have used for a stool, clothes and towels hanging on nails, two rattan chairs pulled close together at a narrow orange-painted table, clear except for an empty vodka bottle. He lived on the floor: the large double mattress, an ash-tray beside it, a lamp, a tape machine and scattered tapes, a small pile of books, an Advocate, a candle melted into a saucer, three pillows, two sleeping bags, a dirty shirt. There was an impression in one of the pillows, the one nearest the ashtray, and she almost saw him lying there, staring at the ceiling and the rising smoke. She stood there a long time, not exactly waiting, eyes on the vodka bottle, caught by a diamond of sunlight in the glass. She would have to talk to that woman. As if suddenly the words—Go talk to

Katie Roberts—were written in big black letters across Spider's bare white walls.

From the restaurant she telephoned Mason. Nothing. No one had called. I hadn't come back. She telephoned Rainy. No answer. She telephoned Jane.

Still asleep, Jane's father said.

Well, get her up. It's important.

What happened yesterday? she said to Jane.

Yesterday? Jane said.

Wake up, Jane. Tess is missing. Get yourself wakened up and meet me at the restaurant. Will you do that? Can you do it fast? Jane?

Sure, Jane said.

But it took her nearly an hour.

Mama sat alone in the restaurant wanting to cry. She drank coffee and smoked cigarettes and needed to talk to Blue. She hated his anger. She hated his leaving. She hated that he didn't have a phone. She was addicted to his skin, to his small hard muscles, to his bones. She liked his smell, his voice, his hesitations. She liked the way he held her, needed to hold her, she liked holding him. She liked his long fingers, the way his mind worked, the ideas he saw in pictures, the stories he told. She liked the way he hid himself inside his body, in his gestures. She liked the ways he let her draw him out. She liked the ways he needed her. She liked needing him. She liked the way their minds sometimes worked together and sometimes worked apart. She liked the opacity, the darkness and silence of his feelings, the suddenness of clarity when they found an image that opened and let clarity break through. She liked to feed him. She liked to be fed. She liked the way when she was with him her mind lived in her body, and her mind—not just her body—made its way into the world. She liked feeling grounded, material, not outside the moment, not beyond it. She took comfort in him, in their conversations, in their stillness, in their sleeping, in their sex. She comforted him. She remembered him playing with wind-up toys, that first Thanksgiving, before they were lovers and barely yet friends, at someone's house full of wind-up toys: walking mailboxes, garbage cans, fire hydrants, telephones, cars with four feet, lumbering plastic elephants, a spider that somersaulted across the room, caroming back from obstacles, somersaulting and dizzy till it wound itself out. She remembered him laughing. He was wearing a pink sweater, she teased him about it, about the color, about the pair of tiny kittens sewn like an alligator over his heart. Back before. A long time ago now. It was true they were not in love, but they had grown a love of some kind and except when he retreated she had thought it a love that was livable, maybe the only realistic love she'd ever known. A love with a built-in distance. A love that demanded reserve. A love willing to be guilty, willing to cause pain, willing to acknowledge causing pain. But she was wrong. Because all along, it was too late. Because now I was gone. Because I would have to go. Because Blue was going. Because last spring, something happened. Adam happened. Everything failed her. Alone in the booth in the restaurant, she sat drinking coffee and smoking, waiting for Jane.

We went to that woman's, Jane said. Spider—you know Spider? He took us there. To get our tarot cards read. But it was only Tess who got her cards read. This woman, you know, Spider's been, well, he's older than we are, he's been sleeping with her. I mean . . .

Go on, Mama said.

She came up to Tess on the meat rack—

I saw them.

She came up to Tess and told her she wanted to read her tarot cards. I mean, you know, she was nice to us. She asked us over, said she wanted to know us, we were Spider's friends. She gave us tea and stuff. And she read Tess's cards. And then we left. I mean, Rainy and I left.

And Tess stayed?

Yeah.

What happened before you left?

Jane shrugged. I don't know. She laid out these cards—you know what they look like?

I know what they look like.

And when Tess was listening to her and looking at them—I don't know, I guess something funny happened. She remembered, or something.

Remembered what?

I mean, I don't know, I shouldn't tell you.

Listen, Jane. It's about Blue. I know it's about Blue. I know what it's about. I want to find Tess. Do you understand me? Jane? I am trying to find Tess. You have to tell me what you know.

Well, if you know—

Tell me, Jane. Tell me exactly.

It was a long time ago, it was last year, last year she used to talk about, about this thing that happened to her at night. Where someone was in her room. You know, touching her and stuff. Sex.

She thought it was China Blue.

Thought?

She said it was. But Rainy and me, I don't know, we didn't believe it exactly. I don't know.

Did Spider know? Before yesterday?

We never told him. I never heard Tess tell him. I don't understand, Holly. Why is she gone?

What did that woman say? When she was reading the cards?

Card stuff, I don't know. Nothing specific, just, I don't know, things.

And Spider took you there? He was there when Tess remembered?

Yes.

What happened when Tess remembered?

Nothing happened. She just said she remembered. I mean, she just remembered. And then Rainy and I wanted to leave. But Tess didn't. I don't know about after. I didn't see her the rest of the day.

I want you to take me there, Mama said. Jane?

I don't understand, Jane said. Why is Tess gone? I don't understand why she's gone.

Well, well, well, Katie Roberts said.

I have to go now, Jane said. This is her, she said to Mama. This is Tess's Mama, she said to Katie Roberts. I have to go, she said but didn't go, stood there waiting as if for someone to tell her what to do.

Come on in, Katie Roberts said. Drink?

Where's my daughter? Mama said.

What? Katie Roberts said.

My daughter. Where's my daughter?

Katie Roberts' face went gold. It went liquid. I wasn't there. But I've seen her face do that. It goes liquid. It goes gold. She says, What? and her face is liquid and gold and you just drop your attitude, you just believe her.

I'm sorry, Mama said. She laughed a little, through the back of her nose, the way she does when she thinks she might be wrong. When she's built up some complex idea of the way things are and suddenly some little moment helps her see she could be wrong. I'm sorry, she said again. I can't find Tess. Can I come in? Can I explain?

I have to go, Jane said again.

Wait, Mama said. Can you go by my house? Take Mason a paper and wait there. Could you call Rainy?

She was going out of town. To her dad's I think. In Providence.

Could Tess be with her?

I don't know. They were leaving real early this morning I think.

Do you know her dad's name? Can you call her?

Jane shrugged. Sure, she said. You want me to buy the paper?

Here, Mama said and pulled her coin purse out of her bag and gave Jane a handful of change.

So have a drink, Katie Roberts said. You're in crisis. You need a drink. People in crisis always need a drink. It's the American way.

Well, Mama said. Maybe I will have a drink.

Vodka, rocks. That's it, Katie Roberts said.

Fine, Mama said.

They sat at the table and looked at each other.

Did you ever ask yourself why so many Americans are alcoholics? Katie Roberts said. I'll tell you. I know the answer to that. I know lots of answers when I don't get enough sleep.

Because we're powerless, she said. Powerless and always in crisis. So have a drink.

She laughed. Uncle Sam, too, she said. The daddy of us all's an alcoholic too. Trying to run everybody's life. Thinks he's God all over the world—see what I mean? But he's just like the rest of us. Powerless too.

She laughed. She shook her head. Her hair flopped all around her face and suddenly she looked up again. She laughed. Liquid and gold.

Sundown on the Union, she said. Know what I mean?

I've known some crazy people in my time, she said, I really have.

You too, she said. I bet you've known some crazy people too.

Then she stopped talking.

Not many people make Mama speechless. But she didn't know what to say back to Katie Roberts.

I tried to talk to her, Mama said. I said, Blue. I said, Your friend. That was all. And right away she knew. This can't be true, I said. But she wouldn't talk to me. In the morning, she said, Mama, in the morning. And now it's morning and she's gone.

On the beach, Mama said, for an instant I knew that I knew. I knew. But I lost it. Whatever it was, I lost it.

I bet you do know, Katie Roberts said.

She's your daughter, Katie said. I bet, I bet if you thought about it, real hard I mean, I bet if you just closed your eyes and concentrated, right now, right now you'd see whatever it is that she's seeing.

You would, Katie Roberts said.

Where's that boy? Mama said. Isn't he here?

Boy? Katie said. Spider? She laughed. Not for hours, she said.

Mama looked at her. She wanted to believe her. She wanted her to be innocent. She didn't know why. She looked away, at the prism hanging in the window, at the child's drawing taped to the refrigerator, at the orange-handled scissors on the table, at the liquid surface of the ice cubes floating in her glass.

What about Adam? she said without looking up.

Adam? Katie Roberts said. Who do you mean? My friend the consummate creep? Anything definite he's ever done he's done out of weakness? That Adam?

Mama didn't answer.

Everything good he's done he's done out of weakness too, Katie said.

If he'd been tougher, she said, you know, stronger, he'd have been a real bad man.

Mama smiled a little. She said, That sounds more like China Blue.

I don't understand, Katie Roberts said. Run it by me again.

What did she tell you? Mama asked her.

A lot, Katie said. It sounded real.

And you won't tell me?

I guess if she'd wanted you to know she wouldn't have disappeared. Now would she?

And you won't tell?

What's to tell? Katie said. She remembered things. She remembered China Blue. You can't expect her to want to tell you about that. Can you? She loves you. She loved him. Think about it. It wasn't something he did to her. She wasn't a little girl. Think of her not as your daughter. Think of her as a woman. A woman who loved you. And desired him. Think of her that way.

But—, Mama started.

But she didn't know what to say. She *could* think of me that way. Sitting there with Katie Roberts, she could. As she had once thought of herself that way. An adult trapped in a child's body. She could think that way. She did think that way. But she didn't know what to say back to Katie Roberts.

Adam lied to me you know, Katie said. He told me he wasn't a photographer.

Mama shrugged. He was trying to give it up, she said.

He told me he never was a photographer, Katie said.

Maybe he wanted to give you what he thought was his best self.

Katie Roberts laughed. You're really in love with him, aren't you? she said.

Yes, Mama said. Yes. I really am.

More vodka? Katie Roberts said.

They tell you you're alone, Katie said, you know? And pretty soon you believe it. And even when it isn't true anymore, you act as if it ought to be. You know why that Tess of yours is going to be all right? Because you let her be. You prepared her for a life alone. And she'll be fine. You know it. Wherever she is, she'll be fine.

She's a little girl, Mama said.

Not so little. You never thought so. And that was good. You forget that now, you're worried. But it was good. You let her grow up for being alone. You let her go. Everyone. You have to let them go.

Want me to tell you how I think it is? she said. I think I'm just like my mother. With her pills and her rich husband and her neglect. I'm just like my mother. I'm just as fucked up and just as alone. I'm following in her footsteps. How I look at it, it's just as well I lost Jesse. You know who Jesse is? Was? My little boy. And I lost him. Because I got . . . incarcerated. And when I got out I didn't claim him back. I let him go. I let him go and he'll be just as neglected by whoever got him as he would have ended up neglected by me. But at least when he realizes he hates those people he won't tear himself to pieces thinking he owes them his life. Me, he can hate me too. He won't owe me either. I'll be the one that wouldn't sober up to get him back. He won't owe anybody anything.

When you're alone at least, she said, you have power over *something*.

But what am I supposed to do? Mama cried. What do you think I'm really supposed to do?

You want to know? Katie Roberts said. Why don't you tell me about it? Why don't you tell me what you think it's like?

What? Mama said.

What, Katie repeated. Losing your kid. Maybe that, losing your kid. Maybe something else. Losing. What's it like, losing?

Mama couldn't answer.

You know what I mean, don't you? Losing? You've lost everything, Katie said. Or hadn't you noticed?

Tess, Mama said. I'm talking about Tess.

She's a little girl. Yeah, you said that already. And I said Tess was fine. Tess went off alone somewhere. Tess will come back. What I'm talking about is you.

No, Mama said.

Katie Roberts shrugged. Maybe not, she said. But maybe if you looked at it straight, you'd get it straight. Know what I mean?

Mama pushed her drink away across the table. Do you have any coffee? she asked.

Not today, Katie said. You think pushing that drink away changes anything? You think coffee changes things?

I should go, Mama said.

That's right, Katie said. You should. But maybe first you should think about a few things. Like who do you love? They're all gone. Aren't they? Why don't you cry? she said. Why don't you cry for them? Doesn't it make you want to cry?

I'll cry later, Mama said. When there's nothing I can do.

Katie Roberts smiled.

You need to cry, she said. It's better if you cry. It's better if you fall apart. Maybe you'd better have another drink.

If you'd interfered, you know, Katie Roberts said, if you'd stopped them from calling the police, none of this would have happened.

What? Mama said.

Maybe she's home by now, Katie Roberts said. Maybe you should go?

What did you say? Mama asked.

I've told you all I can. I think you really should go.

No, Mama said.

No? Katie Roberts said. You don't want to leave?

What did you mean? Mama said.

Shall I call the police? Katie Roberts said.

What?

Hey, take it easy, Katie said. Tess is missing. Do you want the police?

Nothing makes sense, Mama said. I thought . . . You said . . .

What did I say? Katie Roberts asked. Her eyes were bright and hard.

They committed me, she said. You know that, she said. That's what they do. What I say doesn't matter. You see that, don't you? Can't you see that?

Mama took a deep breath. She shook her head no, and Katie smiled and got up from the table and filled a glass with water. She came back and put it in Mama's hands and stood beside her while she drank, and when Mama put the glass down and looked at her again, Katie touched her fingertips to Mama's cheeks and wiped away her tears.

Now you'd better go, she said. I really think you should go.

Mama nodded. She stood up.

That was how Spider found them. He ran up the stairs and knocked three times and opened the door and there they were: standing together at the end of the table, the winter sun making halos in their hair.

See who's here, Katie said to him quickly, and he stopped where he stood.

Do you know where she is? Mama asked.

Who? Spider said, acting confused, looking from Mama to Katie. Tess?

You really don't know? Mama said.

Tess? he said. You talked to Tess?

Mama nodded.

God, he said, disgusted. Mothers.

He crossed the room and sat at the table and stared at the vodka glasses.

Great, he said. Really great. She's not with Rainy and Jane?

No, Mama said.

He wouldn't look at her. He sighed.

I'll have to help you find her, won't I? I got her into this.

You know somewhere she might be?

Maybe, he said. Maybe in the beech forest.

Poor Tess, he said, still staring at the glasses. I should have known better than to talk to anyone's mother.

What did you think? Mama cried. What did you think was going to happen when you came out of nowhere and said what you said and walked away?

Kamikaze, he said. Divine wind. He laughed. His eyes never left the vodka glasses. You bitch, he said. You great, stupid bitch.

Enough, Katie Roberts said. Spider, she's had enough. She doesn't need you calling her names. Leave me your number, she said to Mama. Go home. He'll go out and look. I'll call you. When he gets back, I'll call you. We'll see what we can do.

Mama walked, refusing words. But words came: *This man here fucked your daughter. Get the hell out of here and go look for her. You've lost everything, you great stupid bitch.* She thought she would call Adam. She thought talking to Adam she would begin to understand. As if talking to Adam she would lose her fear. As if with Adam listening, she would know what was real. Fragments from his letter came to her: *I remember a red bandanna shirt you used to wear. I remember the power of believing. We were crazy about each other, Holly. Maybe again.* He wrote to her about light. *You give me light,* he wrote. He wrote about faith and resignation. He wrote about his body. He wrote that he was waiting for a world in which the frightened would not be lonely in their sheets. *I have to stop drinking,* he wrote, *and don't know how and don't know why and this minute am leaving this room to mail this letter and buy another bottle.* It was a letter full of stops and starts, a letter that never ended, just left off.

She found Mason alone at the table, reading The Week in Review.

Any luck? he asked.

She shook her head.

Jane thinks she must be with Rainy, he said. She didn't want to wait.

She isn't with Rainy, Mama said. She sat down. I saw that woman, she said. You know that woman? Who freaked out last year? Who was with Adam all summer?

Why don't you call the police, Holly?

I can't. I told you. Didn't I tell you? I called the police once. In Berkeley, she said. When Tess was a baby. A man got in the apartment in the middle of the night and I woke up and found him sitting at the foot of my bed. I even talked to him for a few seconds, until I was awake enough to know he was real. I screamed and he ran away. When the police came, they made me feel like the criminal. I can't call them. Didn't Jane say anything?

What are you thinking, Holly? What do you think happened?

I think she ran away. She ran away from me. I think she had a good reason and she ran away. I think she's hiding. I think she might come back. But she's afraid. I have to find her. Not the police, Mama said. Me.

Maybe you should go now, she said. *Maybe you understand. Maybe I'll be in New York soon. Maybe I'll see you.* Maybe I need to be alone.

She wanted to call Adam. Talking to Adam she thought she would find the right words, and with the right words she thought she would find me. He had sent her a number where she could reach him when he got to New York. She thought at that number they might know how to reach him in Santa Fe. But when Mason was gone and she looked around the room, she didn't see the letter. She looked through my homework, still spread across the table. She looked in her purse. She went into her bedroom and looked on top the dresser and on the nightstand and on the window sill next to her bed. She came back out and looked again. She called Mason and asked if he could have picked a letter up with his *Times*. While she waited she realized Florida must know how to reach Adam. Mason didn't have the letter. She poured herself a drink, in last night's glass, still on the table. She lit a cigarette. She sat in her chair by the window. Shadows rose from the water.

She remembered Florida, in April, on the phone from the office: Have you stopped seeing that nut yet? Are you coming back to New York? Mama laughed. I hear Adam's up there, Florida said. Have you seen him? Yes, Mama told her. I've seen him a lot. Oh? said Florida. They talked for a while and at the end of the week Florida arrived for a short vacation. Florida who never took vacations. She called Mama from her room at the Holiday Inn. The Holiday Inn, she said, can you believe it? We'll get together, she said. Maybe a movie. They're showing *Manhattan* downstairs in the bar. A few hours later, half expecting Adam, Mama called her to cancel and as soon as she heard Florida's voice knew Adam was there in her room. She didn't mention him. Neither did Florida. They agreed to skip the movie. Mama waited. Adam never came. In the morning, Florida appeared.

Don't say anything, Mama said. I know.

Florida said they were drinking and talking. It just got inevitable. All he was after was a good time.

It doesn't matter, Mama said. It's all right.

It didn't mean anything, Florida said. He's confused. This thing with you's too heavy.

I know, Mama said. It doesn't matter, she said again, and it really didn't, it had nothing to do with her and Adam, or with her and Florida either, she thought, and Florida pulled a joint from her pocket and lit it and they hung out together the rest of the day. They walked the street, from one end of town to the other. They sat in sunny bar windows. They talked and laughed and drank. They said they were playing a chess game. The town was the board. They analyzed the moves. Sometimes they were the players. Sometimes they were the queens being played. They had nothing to do but walk in the sun and drink and talk and wait to be seen. Mama talked about the men she'd loved. She talked about leaving my father. She talked about her own father dying. She talked about Adam. She talked about China Blue. They finished their drinks and moved on to another bar, where Florida talked about her mother and her photographers and about the marriage that failed just before her career took off. All day they walked and talked, Florida big, generous, laughing, until abruptly she quit the game. They were in the Whaler seeing Manhattan and ran into China Blue. Florida left during the second reel. I hate this movie, she said, and Mama went to the phone. I told her Adam was with me, I'd made him some coffee, he was listening to Patsy Cline. Tell him to wait, Mama said. Tell him I'm coming home. She went back to the bar and said it was urgent and asked Blue to drive her, and out on the street when he dropped her off, for the first time in more than a month, she kissed him goodbye.

I talked to Florida, Adam wrote. She asked me where my cameras are. I'm shedding skin, I told her. Shed it on your own time, she said. She wants me back in Salvador. I told her wouldn't go back. I'll never go back. She tried to talk to me about Karen. She tried to talk to me about you. You sound just like Holly, she said. Too good for this world. I've always sounded like Holly, I said, you never listened. And I'm not listening now, she said. You can't quit, Adam. I won't allow it. And I couldn't tell her what I can't even tell you. I can't write about this. I hate myself for this letter. I hate myself for everything in it. It's full of lies. Maybe you understand. Maybe I'll be in New York soon. Maybe I'll see you.

Sitting in her chair by the window, Mama watched the night come on and saw herself in love with Adam for a real long time. She saw imagination become reality. She saw catastrophe come imploding, herself that morning in April walking alone to the Truro line because the night before, when they were all leaving a bar together, Adam had gone with Florida to spend another night. Because the second time it mattered. Maybe not to them.

But to her. Because she woke up knowing she'd cried all night. She got up while I was still asleep and started walking. She walked on Commercial Street, then cut over to Bradford. She didn't want to meet anyone. She walked on Route 6. She saw the sign for entering Truro. She wanted to keep on walking. As if she could quit us. As if all she had to do was walk away.

Ten months later, the night of my disappearance, without leaving her chair by the window, Mama is walking again in chaos toward Truro, toward forever, toward out. She is betrayed. Reality is too full for the mind to grasp. Even her mind. Especially her mind. She walks, everything backward, the world turned inside out. First the rapture, then the fall. An image in a mirror. In that chaos, she knows where I am. In her chair in the dark by the window, she wants to know the heart of that Holly who walks. In the heart of that Holly who walks she will find the Tess she failed to find today. But she can't reach that Holly. That Holly is gone. Mama's the one who turned back (because she couldn't walk away) and faced Florida (because she had to) and knew Adam had really left her, or not so much left as stepped to the side, and was not heartbroken (because nothing could be that simple) and was not even really confused (because everything was transparency itself)—but lost words. Reality had gone too far too fast beyond her ability to anticipate, to comprehend it in advance. To herself, to me, to Mason, to Blue, maybe even to Florida, without explanation she said, If I were a person who gets sick I would get sick now, if I were a person who goes crazy I'd go crazy. But I don't get sick or go crazy and I'm full of whatever it is that makes people do those things, that makes those things happen. She wanted to call it energy. She wanted to call it love thrown back into itself. She wanted to call it imagination that refused to be transformed. But she knew it was not those things. It was too raw. It was chaos. It was the body without words.

It was an ordinary story. But not for her.

In her chair alone by the window she tried to remember. She tried to imagine that chaos, that pain. She tried to imagine me. She couldn't do it. The Holly who left was lost to her. She was the Holly who turned around, the Holly who wouldn't walk out but knew other ways to run and came back and ran—into her body, into her mind, into her will, throwing everything into Blue. To bring Blue out of himself, she'd thought. If not to keep him, then to make herself historical for him. To push him to know what it was for someone to be historical. As if there was no such thing as too late. As if she was not the Holly who saw the sign for Truro and stopped and turned around: She walked all day. In circles. Avoiding going home. Avoiding the phone. Knowing Florida would come by or call. Walking racked on Florida's betrayal, not Adam's. Until, exhausted, she gave up, and five minutes later, on the way to the airport, Florida walked up our stairs.

Mama shook. She couldn't stop the upsurge of sobbing and tears.

Florida stood in the open doorway, stunned at the sight of Mama's broken face.

I didn't want to see this, she said. It gives me power over you.

As if up the Cape Cod highway Mama's ghost wasn't still walking. As if across the canal, somewhere on the mainland, the ghost of her pain wasn't out there running away.

Mama got up from her chair and turned the lights on and began to look for the letter again. She didn't remember whether Adam really had written that the letter was full of lies. She wanted to know. She wanted to hear his voice. She wanted to hear herself talk to him. She wanted to know what she would say. She looked in her purse again. She looked on all the bookshelves, in books she knew she hadn't opened, in the bathroom, in the kitchen, on top of the refrigerator, in unlikely places, inside the refrigerator, in cupboards and kitchen drawers. The letter was nowhere. She went into her bedroom and reached down the sides of the bed where it pressed up against the wall, even though she was sure she hadn't brought the letter to bed. She had read it at the table. The night before. When she was confused. When she read and re-read the letter and kept hearing *I don't know, Mama. Mama, I don't know.* When she couldn't imagine it: me and China Blue.

She came back to the table and looked in her purse again. She had left the letter on the table. She had left her purse on the table. She was beginning to understand. She opened her wallet and found less money than had been there but more than she expected: some ones and a ten dollar bill.

She closed her eyes.

No, she said out loud.

She called Rainy, who still wasn't home.

The telephone rang.

It's Katie, the woman said. Spider didn't find her. I'm sorry about this afternoon, she said. About what he said.

He didn't look for her, Mama said. Or are you lying to him too?

The woman didn't answer.

This isn't over, Mama said. She hung up. She stood by the phone and when it didn't ring again, she lifted the receiver and dialed.

Call me, she said to Florida's machine. It's Holly, she said. Tess ran away.

She hung up and suddenly gagged, as if the wind had been punched out of her. She struggled for air and gasped and took in a breath and cried out, as if Florida could hear her, *Because I loved you too.* She sobbed and threw herself around the table, saying, Tess, you little fool, why didn't you take it all? Blue, she said, grieving. Coward. Fool, and crying and weeping, stumbled from room to room. She saw her face and her body in windows, in mirrors. She covered her eyes, and her mind asked, Who is this performance for?

She shrieked inside her throat. She was helpless against my absence. She had exhausted her possibilities. In her bedroom she stopped moving. She said out loud: Adam isn't God. God is God. She listened to the words. She said out loud: *Our Father, who art in Heaven*. She said, *Hallowed be thy name. Thy kingdom come*. She stopped. She listened. She said, *Thy will be done, on earth as it is in Heaven. She said, Give us this day our daily bread. Forgive us our trespasses . . .* and pausing to listen at every line, went on all the way to the end.

Her body was calm. She had stopped crying.

She dropped to her knees at the foot of her bed and put her hands up in front of her face. She pressed her palms together and closed her eyes.

She began again, astonished: *Our Father* . . .

She raised her head. She listened.

I know where she's going, she said out loud. Where she's gone. I have known all day.

Occam's Razor

The sun rose on the desert, city lights appeared and disappeared, clouds rolled across a barren land. In the lucidity of his drunkenness this is what he knows: that he has to stop drinking; that to stop drinking isn't the only thing, is the first thing, not the end; that the damage he has done continues, opening out behind him, everywhere he's been. He knows nothing happened, he had just kept waiting till he'd used his waiting up. When his credit ran out and he hitched a ride to Santa Fe and called New York collect, the receptionist told the operator to have him leave a number and he drank five hours before the bartender called his name—a long time ago now, weeks, maybe months. He knows time is something else when it stands still. It was seven o'clock in New York and Florida was in her office, watching the news on three networks and pushing for one thing only: I want you back in Salvador. Maybe, he told her and got her to promise to send his mail and sales reports and back payments by certified check, but didn't have an address and told her he'd call again. At the bar he drank and talked to strangers until he found himself at a party where a wispy-haired girl took him to bed and didn't care that he didn't make love to her, or that during the night he called her Karen, called her Katie, called her Holly, or that in that night and in time to come he would never know her name. The house was full of students. They fed him. The girl found him a job in a used bookstore. He tried not to drink, but not drinking made him crazy, made him shake, made him sweat, and everywhere else the world was going on without him. He turned thirty-five and walked the highway toward Taos and a harvest of mushrooms and ultimate light. He carried an open bottle of vodka and drank and walked and told himself that the mind does not distinguish between what it perceives and what it imagines, that in Salvador was the crucifixion, that he had washed his hands, that in Salvador Lucia X was disappeared, Jesús María and Juan Baptista were disappeared, and Lina and Clara were dead along the Pan American Highway; reminded himself that the camera was not a cock, it did not penetrate the body of the world, the photograph denuded the world and emptied the mind, the image fixed in film was a lie, invisibility was the secret, was the terror, was the truth; remembered that in Nicaragua the wind never stopped blowing, that in the campos the children, no longer dying from hunger, polio, and measles, hunted salamanders and lizards with handmade slingshots, and that if the yanqui armies came the children would hunt yanquis too, until he had wandered off the highway and found earth under his hands, between his fingers, in his mouth, rolled over to look at the stars, and in the dense-packed stars heard the voices of the disappeared and his own damaged. He knows Florida Carter will never understand him. He has left the world and nothing he has witnessed is the reason. He has no excuse. El Playón didn't do this to him, not Lina and Clara, not what he's done or what he's failed to do. He didn't even do it to himself. It just is. Like the vodka-lucid darkness and the humming in his head.

He tries to touch his head, but can't move his hands, can't feel his hands, or his heartbeat or the stiffness in his muscles or the location of one part of his body in relation to another. He can't feel his body anywhere, can only hear the humming and remember that he had called Florida back to ask where his money was and she answered Where are your cameras?; that he raged, that he drank; that he called her again, collect from the bar, saying Florida, I want you to understand—but lost what he wanted to tell her and asked instead Where's Karen now?; that Florida told him Back in Salvador and demanded Don't you think this little breakdown can wait? Because you want to know what I really think is Karen went down there looking for you; that he laughed, that he laughed for hours; that he walked back to the house and tried to call Karen while the girl said Great Spanish—he can still see her with her pale wispy hair saying Great Spanish and hears Florida asking What makes you think you can save the world when you can't even save yourself?, saying Booze is like novocaine, it makes you feel huge when all you are is numb, and remembers thinking maybe Florida was finally getting the message, maybe now she'd get off his back—but Karen wasn't in her room and wasn't in the hotel bar, and he was afraid to leave his name and made one up. He tried to finish his letter to Holly. He went to a liquor store and bought a quart of vodka. He walked the road toward Taos until the stars spoke words he knew. *Ba ba ba* the baby says, *ma ma ma, labilee labilee labilee* the babies say, all the babies everywhere, *ba ma ga labilee labilee,* the word, the freedom of the word, the innocence of the word, the poverty of the word, the hunger of the word, the love, all the love was in the word, in the beginning was the word, in the night was the miracle, love was in his empty pocket, and the last thing he remembers is throwing his empty bottle into the star-dense New Mexico sky. He wants to open his eyes. His muscles are cramped, his bones are cold, he needs a drink. He knows he's been dreaming but not the dream. He knows if you open your eyes they blind you. He remembers they stopped the bus. They ordered everyone out and arms up against the metal. His palms burned. Their hands moved over his body. Their hands moved over the bodies of the women. They felt him up and down and up even after they found that all his heavy-hanging pocket concealed was his traveling flask of Nicaraguan caña. They laughed while they shared his rum around and let him take their pictures, but when they prodded him back into the bus, the other passengers after him, they held Lina and Clara and told the driver to drive on. He shook through the rest of his journey. He told himself it was rage for Lina and Clara, rage at the impotence of his cameras, of his imperial passport and press credentials, of his thirty-six shots of Salvadoran soldiers harassing civilians alongside a bus. He knows he told himself lies. He had the shakes for his Flor de Caña and three days later Lina and Clara turned up on the empire's high-way, thumbs and ankles tied, faceless, sliced from ear to ear. He smelled them. He touched them. He turned their dead anonymous bodies into clear, bright images of the terror. His cameras would never stop it. His cameras were not guns, they fed off the evil, fed him off the evil, kept him in Stolichnaya at the Hotel Camino Real and on the road soaked in Nicaraguan rum. He knows nothing will change. He's crossed the line. He needs a drink. He knows if he moves he'll find the bottle that must be with him and if God is good it won't be empty, knows he can't move, but does. The weight that stifles him is his overcoat. He inches it down from his face. He smells diesel fuel, breath, bodies. He smells the city. He opens his eyes. The bus is dark. He gropes with shaking hands wondering where he is and where the money came from and how many days he's lost, thinking he must have robbed the register at the bookstore or prowled the house stealing from the students or maybe the girl, and strikes glass, the bottle lodged between the back of the seat and his left thigh, and knows he has no feeling in his legs but blinking at the pain in his eyes from the lights that pass on the highway sees that God is good, or he's been good to himself, the quart he's loosened from its place of safety but can't yet lift contains almost two inches of 80-proof alcohol, Stoly—that must have been some bank he robbed. Already his feet and legs begin to tingle and unsteadily his hands screw open the cap and together bring the bottle to his mouth to measure out one slow sip and another, enough to enable him to move his feet and legs and drink again, getting strength enough to sit up and look out the window at the empty darkness of an interstate that's already taken him far from the Sangre de Cristo Mountains, determination enough to re-cap the bottle and stash it in the empty seat beside him, and mind enough and fear to begin to search the pockets of his army jacket for information and evidence against himself. Afraid to count his money, he starts with the cards but finds only the usual plastic and paper, his expired VISA card, the phone card, gas cards, American Express, none of them any good now, the blue-and-white New York City library card, Social Security, Karen's business card, printed with the name and address and phone number of the agency, his international driver's license, the headshot rumpled, unshaven, long-haired, vaguely green, and seeing his own image appear and disappear with the highway lights, remembers a moment of panic in front of a mirror when he couldn't find his face: his silent companion had finally left him, or left the mirror, taken over—he the one gone missing now. The panic passed, or didn't, he doesn't remember, all he remembers is a dark room, the empty mirror, an aura. He opens the wallet, smells new money, his fingers freezing on a crisp stack of bills. He sees a bank, mahogany and marble, a shaft of filtered sun, hears himself yelling but not the words. He goes for the bottle and stops to switch the overhead light on, shaking again, and closes his eyes and opens them slowly, holding the money between his knees even though no one is near to watch. He counts. Seven hundred in new fifties and twenties. Two grubby fives and a ten. He reaches for the bottle and drinks. Terrified he folds the new bills and hides them in a different zippered pocket of his jacket, slips the fives and the ten back into the wallet and pulls out the piece of paper he's been carrying there with his money. One afternoon in the store, alone, waiting for customers, baffled, brooding, confused, he left his stool and browsed until he found a King James Bible and took it off the shelf. He closed his eyes, turning the Bible around in his hands until he didn't know what was top or bottom or front or back and let it fall open and pointed blind to the page. He wanted an oracle but when he opened his eyes he saw that his finger had landed in the gutter between the left column of text and the right. On the right he read: *And I have given you a land for which ye did not labor, and cities which ye built not, and ye dwell in them; of the vineyards and oliveyards which ye planted not do ye eat*—which filled him with shame, for his life and his country—and on the left: *And Joshua said unto all the people, Thus saith the Lord God of Israel, Your fathers dwelt on the other side of the flood in old time, even Terah, the father of Abraham, and the father of Nachor: and they served other gods*—which nourished his secret suspicion that his fate and his guilt were bound up with the fate and guilt of the nation, and because he was touched by how directly the two verses seemed to speak to him, fragments of an exhortation addressed to his own obsessions, he tore the page from the book and stuffed it into his shirt pocket and later carried it folded up in his wallet, from time to time when he was drunk enough pulling it out and reading the verses over, searching them for something less transparent, something only vodka would reveal, until the words took shape in his dreams and he caught himself repeating them so habitually that all they can tell him now is what he already knows. He empties his bottle. He says: I'm a thief. Am I a thief? he asks and looks at his reflection. He digs into another pocket and finds his dog-eared passport and an old photo of Karen and one of Tess he bought from some kid on a bus, snapshots of his mother and father he took when he was ten, others of himself and his brother when they were boys, his brother's beautiful wife, his brother's beautiful children, and folded into a small rectangle Karen's full-page color photograph of teenage hookers on 42nd Street that ran just after Christmas in the Sunday magazine of *The New York Times*. Digging deeper he brings up a purple rabbit's foot and a piece of clay pipestem he picked up on the beach in Provincetown and feeling its sand-softened, ocean-worn surface, brings it to his lips, sucks air and wants a cigarette, finds a pack and matches in another pocket and with them the receipt for his bus ticket, Denver to New York. He wonders why Denver and if the bank was in Denver and how he managed it and trembles knowing he's emptied his bottle, he'll be alone now when they take him, listing like accusations what they'll find on his body—the photo of Karen, the photo of Tess, the children, the beautiful woman, the teenage hookers, the rabbit's foot, the empty bottle, the driver's license, the plastic, the money, the page torn from the Bible, the passport stamped with visas from twenty dispossessed countries they think are another world—and laughs thinking soldier of fortune, Bible desecrator, liar, lecher, leaver, and blinks back tears and unzips another pocket and comes up with a torn manila envelope and a fistful of fowarded mail—bills, all unopened, the phone company, VISA, American Express, various collection agencies, a note scrawled from Florida, *Thought I forgot you, didn't you?*, an airplane ticket, Denver to New York, and a moment of vision, a close-clipped man in a blazer shaking his head saying Sorry, sir, and understands that he tried to cash in this ticket but Florida had somehow screwed him or he had screwed himself and sees his hands and a drink in the sunshine in an airport bar and planes flying out and knows he must have sat and watched and waited as if before long he would fly out too but saw the people in the airport and on the ground and at the bar beside him dead and knew he wouldn't fly, and goes for another pocket and comes up empty and another and finds an unopened half-pint of vodka whose weight he's been avoiding for fear it was a gun and blesses his foresight and wonders if this inventory too will evaporate into a single moment or nothing at all and in the same pocket finds a scrap of paper, his receipt for the certified check sent by the agency, by Florida, with his bills, his carbon-copied signature not even shaky, the check drawn on a Denver bank, a thousand dollars, only three hundred gone—the vodka, the bus ticket, maybe his debts paid, some of it lost probably, dropped, given away—and opens the bottle expecting to feel relief but feels nothing, knows only terror and remembers that in his dream he was driving toward Columbus Circle and stopped at the intersection waiting for the light. A cab pulled up behind him. More cabs. Pedestrians stepped in front of his car. Behind him one of the cabs honked. The light changed. All the cabs were honking. If he drove on he would hit the pedestrians. The honking didn't stop. Pedestrians were everywhere and suddenly he ran them down. He wasn't the driver anymore, just a passenger in the guilty cab, and when he got out to help the victims, he found only a body dump—the dead long since abandoned, old meat and bones. He turned away. He was alone. He saw the pale winter trees of Central Park against a white sky and said out loud to no one *My disease is my disease* and pulled his overcoat around himself and couldn't cry. He repeats the word: disease. Out the window he sees refineries and chemical plants laced with colored lights, and in the distance the bright white towers and blue-strung bridges of New York. The bottom falls out of his stomach. He knows where he is now and what he is. He knows he can finish this bottle now. He knows just how close he is to the street.

Tarbabies

Mama waited a few days, in case I showed up, but she knew I wouldn't, she knew I'd gone. Back to where we came from. She packed quick, left our boxes and the cat with Mason, and took the bus to New York. She stayed with Florida and went to work again at the photo agency, cataloging the archive. Nights and mornings, lunch hours and weekends, she walks the city and rides the subways looking for me. She checks shelters and youth services and parks. She's tracked down Spider's mother. She goes from church to church and priest to priest. She's been in the city almost three weeks, has just borrowed money from Florida and moved into a little place of her own, when she gets a call from Blue.

Night after night on the couch, he tells her. Going as crazy as his mother. Trying not to ask what has been done to him—as if, denied words, the question would go away. Waking to the predawn light and his mother's roomers banging down the stairs, out to the boats. And then this: his father, skinless flesh and broken bones, struggling in the salt air and storm-black sea. Dreams of the dead don't stop the killing, he says, giving himself away, echoes of that letter from Adam. He brought this on himself. As if his father had written that letter—from another world, from the desert under the water. As if coming home was exile. As if it were possible, he says to Mama: Tess in my room.

He's thirty years old, he says, and he's had enough. Morning is morning. A couch, a bed. One room, another. Here, there. Alone or with you. What's the difference? The same immobility. The same hesitation. The mindless groping for a cigarette. The need to dig in under the blankets, to wait, to disappear. I didn't do it. Fucked the daughter, read the letter, what's the difference? If it's not one thing it's another.

We were at a Halloween party, remember? he says. You didn't wear a costume. I went as Captain Ahab. You got into my life. I was nothing. You heard me. You heard me call your name. You believed that punk. I have a gun in the trunk of my car, packed into one of my boxes. I brought this on myself. I read that letter. I talked to Katie Roberts. But I never hurt Tess. I never did

At breakfast he's tried to talk to his mother, but his mother is a stranger. He's the roomer who lives on the couch. She wants to know what's wrong with him, what he's running from. But he doesn't know, can't say. He spends days in the attic, going through his old things. He hears his mother downstairs, cooking for the men when they come home from the water, unless they stop in town first to drink. He would like to open their doors, touch the furniture, sit on the beds. He would like to go into his old room and look out the window, a ghost in his mother's own house.

Every evening he wanders down to the kitchen and asks his mother if she wants his help. Maybe Nina and her husband the cop and their children are coming to dinner. Nina is fat and happy now, she has three fat happy children. She's a stranger. His mother served a term on the zoning board. She goes out on dates and makes breakfast for fishermen who live in her children's rooms.

Why don't you peel those potatoes for me? she'll say. I'm going up to lie down.

The window over the sink faces the backyard. No more rusty swing set. No bicycle next to the trashcans, under the second-story stairs. Less garden, more grass, frozen brown. The willow tree looks dead. He runs water over his hands, over the big red dusty potatoes loose in the sink. He finds a stainless-steel bowl and fills it with water. He finds the potato peeler, the kind that fits over the knuckles, the kind he's missed in every house he's lived in since he left his mother's. He peels, meticulous. With a twist of the looped blade, he scoops out the eyes. He rinses the peeled potato and drops it into the water. He picks up another, peels, scoops out the eyes.

He thinks about her while he works, deciding whether to call. In the cold water and deft labor of his hands, he knows. He will. He will call and he will go back. He will make her listen. He will make her understand. He's innocent. She needs to know he's innocent. Tess needs to know. He needs to know.

The blade slipped. His finger bled, bright into the gleaming bowl. He put the potato down and took the peeler off his hand. He went to the phone and hesitated, shaking. He willed himself to pick it up, to dial. Her phone was disconnected. He tried the restaurant. They gave him a number in New York. A machine answered. A woman's voice, not hers. He didn't leave a message. He sat at the table resisting tears. This table. This table where everyone died. Where he sat with coffee cans of crayons, scribbling, coloring, drawing, painstakingly writing his name. The letters of his name. This table where he ate while his brother disappeared in action. This table where he knew before anyone that his father would never come home. He is twenty-three years old again. He is sitting at this table and his life is in shreds on the porch. A bureaucratic accident. A mistake. He got the message. This table where he pounded his white-knuckled fist and cried again and again, I got the message, I got the message, until he heard his mother's car in the drive and went silent and climbed the stairs to his room and threw some clothes into a canvas knapsack and counted his money and picked up his bankbook and keys and came down and watched his mother put away groceries, and when she was done and the bags were folded and stacked in the drawer next to the sink, he told her he had to go, and left the house calling out See you later, and never came back.

Until now.

He sat at this table waiting while one of the roomers went up to get her and in the sound of an indrawn breath he heard his mother's unbearable love. She said his name, so whispered he almost didn't hear it. He looked up and into her face and knew he was the one who would cry. She stood in the doorway. She couldn't come nearer. He was an apparition. From another dimension. She didn't believe him, his distance, the years. He wanted to vanish. But tears spilled down his eyes and he said Mommy like a six-year-old. She rushed to his side and held his head to her belly, stroking his hair, saying Daniel, Daniel, giving him back his name, Daniel Matthew Santos, that Catholic, Portuguese name that had never made sense of him or his body—so slight, so arid, strung so tight on long, old Puritan bones. Stop, he said, but he didn't move. Daniel Santos. Son of Richard. Brother of Bobby. Brother of Nina. Baby of the family. Sole survivor. Going home.

But he was not the sole survivor. He was a stranger when his brother died and every time he left and returning he was a stranger still.

He tried calling Mama again, left a message.

It wasn't hard to find you, he says.

They don't need me here, he says. It's almost over. He knows it's almost over. He shouldn't have run away.

I shouldn't have run away, he says.

Mama doesn't answer.

I was angry, he says. Because you believed that kid. I want to come back.

She says, I just saw a girl on the subway take a big school book out of her bag and I remembered what it was like when I was young and loved ideas and believed ideas could bring some goodness into the world. How's your mother?

Holly, he says. Did you hear me?

She doesn't answer.

I was angry, he says. Is that so hard to understand?

I don't know, she says. I don't know if I want to talk about it. How are you doing? How's your mother?

I just told you how my mother is. My mother's fine. I'm here and the days go by. Badly. Holly, I miss you.

I have a job again, she says. Florida put me back to work. I had to have something.

I'm looking for Tess here, she says.

I'll help you look. I want to come back.

I never told you to leave.

I was angry, he says again.

She doesn't answer.

I didn't do it, Holly. Did Tess say I did?

I don't know, she says.

I didn't. I swear it, Holly. It was someone else. Some other time. Some other place. It wasn't me.

Do you believe me, Holly?

When I was fourteen, she says, I used to want to run away.

You have to believe me, he says.

I used to hear the train whistles from my bedroom, she says. I used to think I could go and hop a train. If only I was a boy, I thought. I used to think I didn't have the courage. It wasn't the being alone I was scared of. That was what I wanted I thought. I imagined the train and I imagined the people on it with me, an old man and a kid with a dog, riding a freight car, all of us running, just going, on and on, out, into the world. Being out there wasn't what scared me I thought. What scared me was the leaving. I didn't think I could do it. I thought the only way I could leave would be to have to—to get pregnant and have to run away. I wasn't even looking at boys then, but that was how I pictured it, and six years later I did get pregnant and got married and after a while I took Tess and ran away from marriage too.

She's the only person I've never run away from, she says. In my life, she says. And now she's run away from me.

She needs help, Blue says.

I'm trying to find her, she says. She's here. Sometimes I feel her watching me.

I'll drive down and join you, he says. We'll find her together. Holly?

I don't know, she says. I'm so confused. I thought I could never be this confused again.

I have to do something differently, Blue.

I have to do something different.

Ground Zero

We are on the bed, in T-shirts, watching King Kong. For three days, the city has been warm. Spider's leaning against the wall, his legs out straight beside me, under the sheet. I'm lying on my belly, propped up on my elbows. During the commercials, he tickles my toes and feet.

He thought Katie Roberts had some kind of plan. She didn't. She flew by the seat of her pants. She said there were certain times of the month when women get psychic. There were atmospheric conditions. With her, there was always the alcohol. We never knew what combination would set her off. She never knew. But she did know I would climb her stairs that night. She even made a bet with Spider. And she won.

Mama is here. I have seen her. I see her from a distance. I see her getting thin.

Spider and I are living in an unfurnished floor-through on Third Street, between C and D. There's a kitchen at one end and a bathroom with a door. We have south-facing windows. We get sunlight all day. Today is so mild we have the windows open and music rises up with the noises from the street: *If you make your bed in Heaven, he's there. If you make your bed in Hell, he's there. He's everywhere.* A breeze billows the curtains, cut from an old sheet. It must have been white once, but now the curtains are yellowed and the room and the bed and our bodies are gold. When I lived downtown with Mama I was afraid of this neighborhood. I never walked here. I walked around it. Now the dealers on the street know who I am. A few of the youngest flash *Hi there* and *¡Hay que cute!* and the rest just leave me alone. At first they watched us, until they saw we don't have money, we live here and we don't buy. They know we aren't narking. The old Puerto Rican women and the children smile. Lie down with me, Spider said the first night we spent here. I think it will be easier if we lie down together a while, and we made a nest of T-shirts and sweatshirts in a corner on the floor. He held my head against his shoulder and he listened to the street noise. I said, I feel like a stranger, a tourist. As if I'm in a foreign country. He laughed. He said, A pale imperialista, killing time in someone else's world. Close your eyes, he said, I'll tell you a story, and even after we both were sleeping he murmured in my ear.

During the morning rush hour in midtown I pass out handbills for spiritual readers, Madame Sophie and Mrs. Smith and a Cuban named Orlando. They promise to remove all evil habits and turn darkness into light. Known for their honesty and integrity, they will help solve all life's problems and bring anyone who wants it peace of mind. They're available for parties. When the handbills are gone I walk in Central Park. I would like to stop and look at trees and watch the pigeons and squirrels. But I have to walk quickly. As if I'm an ordinary kid, who has a job or goes to school. As if I have a destination.

Look at him, Katie Roberts said in our room on 47th Street. Older than time and younger than the world. She sat down beside me and drank. Spider was curled up sleeping in the single bed he shared with her. Katie was pacing. The night was blue. I was asleep on my folding cot until I heard her talking. Alma was my mother's name, she said. Alma—and her body shriveled up and lost intelligence. I saw my father on the street today. I wanted to spit in his face. I wanted to tell him someone should form Capitalists Anonymous. You know: We are powerless over history; the world has become unmanageable. She laughed.

Did you really? I said.

Did I really what?

See your father.

My father? she said. She started to cry. My father, she said. She shook her bottle toward Spider's sleeping body. Look at him, she said. Older than time and younger than the world.

She sat down and drank. I went to those meetings, you know. In the loony bin they made me.

Every day I try to call Adam, she said. Every day they tell me he isn't here.

I lost everything for him, she said. She cried some more and babbled.

She wasn't really unhappy, she was only talking.

A few days before we left her, Spider took the L-train out to Brooklyn to visit his mother and brought me back a shopping bag filled with his old clothes. He got this place month-to-month. His mother gave him the up-front money but only on condition he'd find a job. She made him promise to think about school. He didn't tell her I was with him, or anything about Katie. He wondered what his mother knew. She would have talked to Rainy's mother, maybe even to Mama. But she didn't ask questions. She has confidence in him. The day he went out to look for a job he came back with the television and a bag of Doritos, a hunk of cheese, a pack of lunch meat, two oranges, a Coke, a flip-top box of Marlboros, and a pile of spare change. He said if he went to school he'd spend half his life paying off student loans. In the apartment below us the super plays piano. The music comes up through the floor. Sometimes I lie here and listen and Violet spreads herself across my belly and purrs. At first we had nothing. The super found us the mattress. He found the curtains. He's a young guy. His name is Tim. He paints still lifes and plays his piano and collects rent for the owners and works on things in the building that wear out or break. He likes us. He brought us a spider plant to hang in the kitchen window. When Violet was a bleeding stray I brought in from the rain he said he'd help me buy her food. Some days I sit for him while he paints me and he gives me a sandwich and one to take up for Spider. He came here from Colorado. He has a big mustache, like a cowboy. Now Spider says I have to leave here, he's enlisting in the Navy. He tells me to go back to Mama. Next to my head Violet purrs. When the curtains billow silver motes shape the shifting light. The dealers shout in the street. Tim plays ragtime. King Kong saves the blond woman from the prehistoric bird.

Every day I look for ways to raise money. I pass out handbills. I ask for quarters at subway token booths. I work one stop a while and walk and work another. Sometimes I work the movies. The early show. A regular kid who has to get home in time for dinner. If someone gives me a token I save it for bad weather and if I have to, I sell it to Tim. I move around. City Corp, Rockefeller Center, Columbus Circle. Sometimes when I get tired I go into Saint Patrick's Cathedral or Saint Bart's and get down on my knees as if I know how to pray. Sometimes I go to the 42nd Street library and when I have a few extra quarters I go into the Met. I like the feeling I get in those old buildings. It isn't so hard to go out and beg after being inside those buildings. Sometimes I stop on the sidewalk and talk with the real beggars. The legless man on the corner of Lexington and 58th. The blind man outside Bloomingdale's. We don't say much. We talk about the weather and what mood people are in. I give them one of my quarters. They think I'm just a schoolgirl, a little bit curious, a little bit lonely, a little bit shy. One time when I was talking to the blind man, Katie Roberts walked by. She didn't know me. She talked crazy on the street.

In her kitchen that night in Provincetown she cut off my hair while Spider watched. I told them I wanted to burn it. They stayed awake with me. Spider told me they'd join me later and sent me down to catch the morning bus alone. When I got here, I walked around a while and went to a movie. I fell asleep. It was dusk when I left the theater. I went back to Port Authority. I sat on the ledge along a big dark window, next to a young black man who was reading a paperback book. I saw my close-cut hair in the glass. It was hard to see my face so naked. Without my hair, my face was bony. My ears stuck out. My eyes were bigger, my cheeks narrower. My face was a stranger. I smelled the sweet dead smell of my burning hair. I looked at the young black man. He wasn't reading. He was writing in his book. His ballpoint pen was red. He didn't turn the page. He covered it with ballpoint ink, wearing it so gossamer thin it curled up red and floated away.

I bought a cup of coffee at the Arby's where Spider said to wait. A policeman gave me the eye. I sat at a dirty table, in a corner by the inside window. A woman came up and asked me did I have place to sleep.

I looked at her like a rock.

She said, You've been sitting around here for hours.

I said, I'm waiting for friends. They missed their bus. They're on their way.

She nodded. She didn't believe me.

It's okay, I said. Thanks. I'm just waiting for them.

She said, How long do you have to wait?

I said, A few more hours.

She said, Want something to eat?

I said, This is plenty.

She said, It's only coffee.

I said, It's not your business.

She said, You're right. I'm sorry. What's your name?

I watched her, trying to decide if I had to tell. She looked like a grade-school teacher. Third grade. She had brown hair, not long, not short. Her eyes were blue. She was very clean. Her makeup was almost invisible. She wasn't wearing jewelry, but her nails were polished, shiny and pale. I told myself she probably only ate health foods. She probably liked Frank Sinatra and maybe the Beatles but not much else. She didn't smoke cigarettes. She never did drugs or drank. She never rode a Greyhound bus. It was hard to figure what she was doing in the Port Authority Arby's with me.

You looked like you might be in trouble, she said.

It's still not your business, I said.

She said well in a way it was. She was a volunteer at a shelter for homeless kids. She said she was here to help kids like me.

I said, I'm not homeless.

Where do you live? she said.

Downtown, I said. I had my library card, with our old address on Church Street.

What's your name? she said.

I told her China Blue.

Great name, she said.

My mother's a kind of artist, I said. You know. Imagination.

Where downtown? she said.

I said, It's not your business.

Not if you're telling the truth, she said.

She shouldn't have said that. Her face changed. She knew she'd made a mistake. I'd made one, too. The library card was useless now that I'd given her a phony name.

I always tell the truth, I said.

Right, she said. She was tougher than I thought. Look, she said, if you need anything, if your friends don't show and you can't get home, you know, it's getting pretty late. You take this card. You take this number. You come by. We can help you.

I said, Honest. It's not that late. I don't need it.

She said, Keep it. She tried to lighten up. She said, If you don't need it, give it to someone who does.

She left it on the table. I didn't pick it up.

As soon as she was gone a woman in layers of rags came asking was I going to use my containers of cream. I gave them to her and two more that were on the table when I sat down. I gave her the packets of sugar and all of my change. I went out to the newsstand and bought a magazine. I went back to sit on the ledge. The same young man was covering a new page with red ballpoint ink. I did puzzles, I read science fiction stories, I read about the mind, about the body, about space, and about the stars. I went back to the Arby's and bought a fish sandwich and took it to the same table in the corner by the indoor window. The card was still there, next to the pie-tin ashtray. I sat down. The biggest lie I told that woman was the lie about my name.

Where's Katie? I asked when Spider walked in with his duffel bag and sat down.

She's coming tomorrow, he said. She wasn't ready. How you doing?

I shrugged.

He picked up the card from the youth shelter and went to a phone. He came back asking did I have any New York ID.

A library card, I said. A school card with my picture from sixth grade.

We'll try, he said. He made up a story. I was his sister. We couldn't stay at home tonight because our father was so drunk. He was afraid he'd kill him. Or our father would kill me. We had different last names because our mother remarried. We could go home tomorrow, when the old man settled down.

What about the addresses? I said. What if Mama's called the

police?

We moved, he said. She hasn't. She won't. Come on, let's go.

We stopped at a phone booth and he called his mother. When she answered he didn't talk, but let the receiver hang down. He fed a bunch of quarters into the phone. He tore a page from my magazine and wrote OUT OF ORDER in thick black letters across the page. He scrunched it into the phone-booth door and left the door almost closed. He said, If nobody hangs up that phone her line will be busy. If they get her anyway I'll make sure they think she lies.

At the shelter Spider did the talking. I didn't see the grade-school teacher. When they talked to me apart from him, I put terror in my eyes. I looked at my hands and mumbled. I even cried.

They took us to separate rooms, and alone in the dark with half a dozen sleeping cast-out and runaway girls, for the first time since leaving Mama, I was afraid. I listened to their breathing and heard nightmares. I heard the street.

Katie was drunk and Spider was drunk. I was awake on my cot in the dark when they came in. Jesse's daddy, she said. You want to know who Jesse's daddy was? I can talk for you Jesse's daddy. It goes like this—

But she stopped talking. Lights from the cars on the West Side Highway swept in and out the window. She made noises in her throat and clicked glass against her teeth. I heard her swallow. I sat up on my cot.

I can't, she said. I can't do it anymore. I don't remember.

Spider was standing at the window, watching the cars.

Psycho, Katie said. Jesse's daddy was nothing, he was no one, he was dead. She saw me sitting up. Escape, Tess, she told me. I don't want to be here. I don't know what I've done.

Suddenly her mood changed. Her eyes opened, big and inspired. Her smile spread wide across her face. She laughed. She came over and sat on the floor and handed me a globe-shaped glass. It still had liquor in it. She must have walked out with it from whatever bar they'd been drinking in. She said, Ronrico 151, and struck a match. She lit the rum in the glass in my hands and took it back.

What color is it? she asked me.

Blue, I said.

She nodded. Like your lover, she said. You don't need him. Forget that man. In your body, this is what happens. This is your lover, sweetheart. Burning alcohol.

Maybe for you, I said.

She laughed. She called me precious and put her hand over the glass to smother the flame. She said, Get out of here. Go save someone else. That, or we'll put you to work.

From the window, Spider said, Katie—

She waited for him to say more, and when he didn't, she drank. She said, Well what am I going to do? Get a job in an office? She laughed.

You could go back, he said.

She snorted. Come to bed with us, she said to me. We'll teach you a thing or two and trade you on the street.

Spider hit her. He threw his body at her and knocked her to the floor. Blood came out her mouth. She made sounds, not laughing, not crying. Animal sounds. Short sobs gasping up high in her chest. He stood over her and offered her his hand. He said, Shhh,

shhh, and helped her to the bed and I lay down and covered my head and heard him kissing her and petting her and getting out of his clothes. Awake, I listened to the slapping of their flesh together and Katie still sobbing and the breathing their bodies made and all I wanted was to be alone in that room with China Blue.

Violet is black. She has yellow eyes. She lost her tail in a street fight or an accident. Unless someone cut it off. Her stump was bleeding the night I found her. She's already getting fat now. The stump of her tail is two inches long and the wound is almost healed. Tim helped me clean it with peroxide and alcohol. From the stores, when Spider shoplifts, he brings her cans of sardines.

I write a letter to my dad, in Tucson, as if I've moved back to New York with Mama, as if nothing's wrong. When Father's Day comes, I'll send him a card.

Tess, Tess, Spider whispered. I was crying into my blankets, as quietly as I could. I thought he was asleep. Hush, he said. He held my shoulders. He pulled me up and held my head against his chest.

I can't stand this, I sobbed.

I smelled her perfume and her body. His hands were hot and gentle on my short-cut hair.

I thought you were asleep, I said.

Katie is. She's passed out.

I thought you were both asleep, I said and I couldn't stop sniffling.

Hush, he said. We'll get out of here. We'll leave her.

Go to sleep now, he said, and in the morning when I woke up

he was already gone.

Where the fuck is he? Katie asked, rolling over. She covered her eyes with both hands against the light.

I shrugged.

She said, Come get in bed with me.

I didn't move.

Her eyes looked bruised and puffy. She pushed her lower lip out. She said, Well, little ice maiden, what do you think I'm going to do?

We could get up, I said. We could go for a walk. We could have some breakfast.

We stink, she said.

We can wash, I said.

The water's cold, she said.

It's better than nothing, I said.

She laughed.

She sat up and pulled her robe on over her head and left the room.

When she came back she had an open bottle of vodka and a little white paper bag. I asked her where she got the money.

An easy trick in a diner john. Here, she said. She tossed the white bag at me and climbed back into bed.

I said, You're lucky you didn't get busted.

She said, The guy was a cop.

Come sit with me, she said, and this time I went. She put one arm around my shoulders and used the other hand to drink.

What happened, she said, is I went up the hall to use the bathroom and found a dollar bill in a corner of the cruddy floor. I thought I might as well get some coffee and bring you a donut. I was sitting at the counter down there barefoot waiting for the waitress when this cop sits beside me and puts his fingers on my wrist. I couldn't smile. I said Leave me alone. My man beat me up. He said Let me buy you some coffee. I said I've got my own dollar. He said I'll buy it for you anyway. I said You want to see the rest of my bruises? He blushed. He said What do you mean? Then I smiled at him. When they blush it's a dead giveaway—remember that, kiddo. I leaned a little closer to him. I put my tit against his arm and made sure he felt it. I watched his groin get big and hard. I said Are you alone in here? He said his partner was out on the street, waiting for the coffee and donuts. I said Meet me in the john. I figured he was young, he was foolish. He said Who beat you up? I said Not a pimp. I'm not a professional. He blushed again. I opened my thigh and bumped him with my knee. I said I could meet you in the john. He laughed. He said Sorry. But I could already feel his fingers up my crotch. I could taste the vodka. I stared at his lips. I said Come on, it'll make me feel like a new woman. I reached for his hand and put it inside my thigh. In my thigh I could feel his pulse beat. He said Don't do this here. I smiled. I said Meet me in the john.

She went on and on. Making it up as she went along. I stopped believing there ever was a cop. I didn't care how she got the money. Listening to her made me want to cry. I ate my donut. I asked for a sip of her vodka and she passed me the bottle.

Now you're cooking, she said, but I hardly drank any. I got up off the bed and said, I'm taking a walk.

I walked downtown, all the way to Battery Park. I stood at the rail and looked at the Statue of Liberty. The sea wind stung my cheeks. Gulls were dense in the air. The water was green. In the financial district I bought a hot dog and spare-changed a few old men to get another. It was cold outside.

I pretended I was a student and sat in the gallery of the stock exchange watching the action on the floor. When I came back to the room Katie was gone. The empty bottle lay on the bed, next to her robe. I stood at the window watching the sunset and traffic. I pulled the chain for the light and sat on the bed and read the Times I'd picked out of a trashcan. I was half asleep when I heard footsteps at the door. Let it be Spider, I thought, and he stood there with a pizza box and a shopping bag full of hand-me-down clothes. He grinned when he saw I was alone. He said, We're celebrating, and we sat on the floor, eating a big double-cheese pizza covered with greasy peppers, and then he took me to a movie. When we came back we heard a man's voice with Katie's in the room. We waited downstairs in the diner, drinking Cokes. A few more days, he said. I'll get her to welfare or something. She'll never make it on her own.

In the bodegas I search the bins of old, bruised produce, looking for the freshest wilting vegetables, the most vaguely damaged fruits. I eat the meats and cheeses Spider steals in other neighborhoods. We watch movies on the television he lifted in broad daylight from an unlocked car. I walk to the Strand and read in the store and sometimes I buy a 20-cent book. I borrow books from Tim and sometimes he brings me one from the library. He says I can't go on like this. He says he's been watching. He says Spider is no good for me. I tell him he doesn't know where I came from. He says that's true but wherever it is, maybe I should go back.

Packed in against the door of the Lexington express, I look out the window at a local train leaving on the track across the platform. In the tunnel the tracks run close together and I watch the local's windows glide along beside me, bright and yellow and full of faces in the dark. I see Mama sitting in the other train. Her face is blank. We move along together, as if the trains are standing still. She raises her head, almost looking at me. Then the difference in our speeds increases, the local slowing for its stop at 23rd, and Mama and the faces and windows blur away from me and disappear.

One morning Spider went out for coffee and came back with a bottle and drank with Katie all afternoon. I lay on my cot, trying to read. Outside it was raining. Don't leave, he said when I got up to go. You're staying in today, he said. Read out loud to us if we bore you. Katie doesn't want to talk anyway, she just wants to drink. Don't you, K? He handed her the bottle. Read, he said. I looked for my place in the book. In the room next door a crazy man talked to the walls. The window leaked. *Sometimes*, I read, *while meditating on these things in solitude, I've got up in a sudden terror, and put on my bonnet to go and see how all was at the farm.* Katie laughed. Keep reading, he said. I went on, and after a while Katie was crying. I know that book, she babbled. I don't want to hear that now, and Spider tried to soothe her, tucking her under the covers, holding the end of the bottle for her while she drank. I was a little girl once, she said. My name was Catherine too, and she put her head down in his lap and, sobbing, begged him to love her. Read, he said and stroked her face and hair while her breathing got deeper and slower until finally she'd passed out. Keep reading, Spider said and slipped himself from under her and packed our things into his duffel bag. Anything else? he asked. Give me the book. *There was no moon*, he read while I went through Katie's purse to find Mama's letter, *and everything beneath lay in misty darkness; not a light gleamed from any house, far or near—*, and at the front desk on the way out he bought another week for Katie in that room.

From now on we are waiting. We don't know for what. Or we think we know but what we think isn't it. Time has to pass. Our blood hurts. Our bodies hum. To be alive is to go down a road you don't know where it leads to. To take a step whose end you can't foresee.

In Grace Church I see Adam, hunched up looking homeless in a shadowed pew.

The first day the sun comes out, walking on St. Mark's Place, I see Mama at a sidewalk table drinking margaritas with China Blue. Bright ferns dangle from the awning poles. Hot-house fuchsias, red in their closed buds, swing back and forth in the late March breeze. A fortuneteller, the Cuban, Orlando, is reading Mama's palm. Blue is smoking a cigarette. Patches of sunlight flutter across their faces. The waitress brings another tray of frothy ice-green drinks, and I'm more afraid for Mama than I ever was for me.

The blind man outside Bloomingdale's laughs when he hears my voice. He calls me Lucky Lady. I tell him my name is China Blue. He says, I know who you are. You smell like lilacs. What's God doing putting you out on this street? I don't know how to answer him. I say I don't guess God had a lot to do with it, and he laughs and finds my hand. He says, China, that's a pretty name, Lucky Lady. The street's not such a bad place. The Lord's gonna work somebody some good with you. You need any help, you come to me.

Spider says he never meant to live like this. He never meant to be a beggar and a thief. He says he's leaving. He's buying into the system. He's joining the Navy and if they won't have him he'll try the Marines. I say he never meant to do that either, learn to kill and be a hero for the rich men that think they run the world. He says it doesn't matter. He has to do something. Fast. There's nothing special here. He says he knows that now. He says, Go back to your mother. I don't know what to do. What about Violet? I say, and he holds my shoulders and looks at me. Shit, he says and pulls my head against his chest. I know he's going to leave me as suddenly as we left Katie. I know he doesn't want me to see his tears. Violet meows. The movie starts. Downstairs Tim is playing ragtime. King Kong saves the little blond girl from the prehistoric bird and the little man shows up to save her from King Kong. Caught by the monster, they fall to safety in the water. King Kong killed the dinosaur to protect her and didn't harm her. He killed the giant lizard and still she doesn't understand.

Street Music

The man grabs my wrist. Tess, he says. It's Tess, isn't it?

He's trembling. He's trying to see my face. He doesn't let go.

Don't be afraid, he says.

I look at his stubbly chin. I look at his eyes. Big and deep-set, pale blue. The man is Adam.

Outside, it's night. It's April and it's snowing. On the laundro-mat benches two winos snore. Another sleeps below them on the floor. I'm somewhere off Delancey Street. I lost track walking. I don't know where I am. In a far corner of the big bright yellow room a fat Latina folds diapers. She hums a little song. Someone is actually doing laundry. Here. Now. In the middle of the night. Somewhere there's a baby who lives in those diapers. Diapers, I think. I think I remember diapers. I remember Mama saying she must have been the last woman in the USA to wash and fold and reuse diapers.

I shake, deep in my belly. Adam's hand still clutches my wrist. I start to cry.

The more homeless I am the less homeless I look. I learn the tricks. I learn the manner. I belong to the streets. When Spider left, Tim had to find a new tenant. He couldn't let me stay. He was afraid to give me shelter. He figured I was underage. He knew I must be a runaway. When I go back to visit him, he tells me I should go home. Home isn't there anymore to go back to, I say. Violet purrs in my lap. Tim paints me while we talk—quickly, in watercolors, page after page. He feeds me an omelette and toast and hot chocolate. He lets me trade a dirty shirt for a clean one I left behind. He says, Wait. Your jeans too. He smiles. He says, I'll be your laundryman. Come sit for me when you need a change of clothes. I hide in my usual places, in churches, in libraries, in the park in the late afternoon. I read, as serious as a student. I keep myself clean in public bathrooms, in museums when I have the money to pay the admission and on evenings when they're free. I move around. I pass out handbills. I spare-change for quarters outside the Met and the Guggenheim, the Whitney, the Frick. I buy a carton of yogurt for breakfast and sometimes a banana. For lunch I buy a bagel, or a hot dog on the street. What's left at night I spend on food unless I have enough to go to a movie, and I sleep wherever I can. I work the subways. When someone gives me a token, I ride. If I have to I can make myself invisible. I can sit there as if I'm sleeping and open my eyes on another world.

It's Solomon who tells me to find a laundromat. Maybe in Chelsea, he says, maybe in the Village, maybe on the Lower East Side. Maybe a diner, he says. Maybe there aren't any all-night laundries anymore. Nobody'd use 'em but people like you. Downtown, he says. Downtown's a desert at night. Nestle in somewhere and hide your face. If no one sees how young you are, they'll leave you alone. Find a steam grate and you'll sleep like the Queen of Sheba.

He laughs. He says, Believe Solomon, Solomon knows. Stay away from the winos, he says. They're harmless but they stink. I tell him I've been sleeping in the weeds at the end of Water Street, under the Brooklyn Bridge. He says it's getting cold, winter isn't really over, it's going to snow again, I should get indoors. I say there are abandoned buildings, stray cats. Maybe if I follow a cat, I'll find my way in. Go to a shelter, he says. I can't risk that, I say. He says, We live in a world that kills heroes, Lucky Lady, even little ones. They don't want us coming back bringing our visions. You don't get redeemed until you know what damnation is. Original sin's not enough. Islam means submission, he says. When the snow starts take a dime and call AA. Find out where there's a meeting. They won't ask questions. You can drink hot coffee and eat cookies and get warm for an hour or two while your feet dry out. Here, he says. Take some of these coins, Lucky Lady. Go buy us a slice of pizza. He laughs. He says, We're a city full of exiles. Millions, we shall eat.

In the crowd at Charlie's Pizza I see China Blue. I watch his face. He's drinking a Coke or a root beer. He's looking out the window at the people passing by. Maybe listening to the conversations of the strangers at his table. I stand at the window counter, waiting for my slice. I wait for China Blue to meet my eye. When he sees me he's not sure. If I weren't staring he wouldn't know me. He looks confused. He stands up. I don't move. When he's close enough to hear I say, I have to take this pizza to the blind man. Tess? he says. Wait, I say, and he lets me lead him along the sidewalk through the crowd. Thanks, the blind man says. You got someone with you? Don't abandon Solomon's porch, he says. Stay and talk to me, Lucky Lady. But I walk on as if he's crazy. I don't want China Blue to know that Solomon is my friend. If he knows, he could come back and try to use him to find me again. We walk east on 58th Street and go into the Blarney Stone. You want something? he says. Lasagne? Roast beef? Roast beef, I say. Whole wheat. He gives me a ten for the sandwich and turns toward the bar. If you go near a phone, I tell him, I'm running. I pocket the change. I wait for him at a little table next to the wall. He brings me a Coke. He comes back with his bottle of Beck's and an empty glass. He sits down. He spreads his fingers on the bright red cloth. I see his bones. His skin is white. His veins are lavender. If I look at his face he'll disappear.

I like your haircut, he says. It should be pink or something.

I don't respond.

I'm surprised you didn't turn your back when you saw me. I wouldn't have known you, he says.

I've seen you before, I say. More than once. With Mama.

We've been looking for you.

Have you told her the truth?

We've searched all over the city. Every night and every weekend.

Have you told her the truth yet?

You have to come back with me, Tess.

Have you told Mama the truth?

He sighs. He doesn't answer.

I didn't want her to know, I say. I didn't want Spider to tell her. I was angry when he told her. I never wanted her to have to know. But it's different now. Why can't you understand that? Now she has to know the truth.

You have to stop saying this, Tess. It's not the truth. You have to come back.

You're talking to me now, not to Mama.

Tess, it didn't happen. Nothing happened.

And she believes you. *This cannot be true*, she says and then she just believes you. Does she think I lied? Or I'm crazy or what?

She doesn't think anything. She just wants to find you. She thinks you need help. I think you need help. You need help, Tess.

Help? What kind of help do you both think I need?

Tess, it didn't happen.

He reaches across the table for my hand and I pull away before he can touch me. The pulse beats in his throat. His eyes are black and empty. He doesn't speak.

You're not lying, I say. You don't even know you're lying.

Tess, you need help.

Not the kind you mean, I say. You don't know, do you? You really don't know.

He hits the table, once, with his fist, and gets up and goes to the bar for another beer. When he comes back his voice is quiet. He says, Why did you run away?

To go where I was believed, I say.

To that woman? That boy? Is that who believed you? That slut and her teenage fuck? What are they doing to you, Tess? You don't belong with them. What are they making you do?

Nothing, I say. They're not your business. I left town alone.

They left too.

They helped, that's all. They know what's true.

And what is that exactly? Why don't you tell me, precisely, in detail, what you think I don't know I've done?

You came into my room, I say.

Once. Yes. I did. I looked at your face in the dark. You were sleeping.

No, I say. You came into my room. You thought I was asleep. I was uncovered. The blankets were flung all sideways. My T-shirt was pulled up around my waist. You touched me. You touched a nipple through my T-shirt and felt the flesh get hard. I was afraid, but that wasn't all. I kept my eyes closed. My legs were open. I had no panties on. My T-shirt was bunched up around my waist. You touched me, Blue. You thought I was asleep and you put your fingers on me. Your fingers were hot. Your fingers felt good and they made me afraid. I got wet. You felt me get wet. I wanted to touch your hand. But you took your hand away. I wanted to tell you to come back. I wanted to cry for help. I wanted to tell you to stay. You brushed your hand against me and pulled away. Something broke open inside me. I opened my eyes. *Shut those eyes*, you said.

His face goes pale. He shudders.

If you see me in here, shut those eyes.

You remember, don't you? You do remember.

I never touched you. I never talked to you. I covered you up and went back to bed.

I saw you, Blue. I saw your body. When I opened my eyes I saw you.

His hands are fists on the table. His face is twisted. It's a face I've never seen. Go on, he says. Let's hear the rest.

I saw your cock, I say. It stood straight up. I was afraid. But I wanted to touch it.

He stares at me. His eyes are glass. He waits. He doesn't blink.

I wanted to kiss you. I wanted—but you told me to close my

eyes and you went away. I watched you leave my room. I wanted to touch your skinny white legs. I wanted to hold your bony shoulders. I wanted to press my face into your marble-perfect ass. But most of all I wanted to pull you back by the hips and turn you around and rub my cheeks and lips against you—

Stop, Tess. What's happening to you? Where do you get this talk?

I wanted you, Blue. Like a woman wants you. I didn't know what I wanted. I wanted everything. I grew. I was air. I was colors. I was light. I filled the room. I thought it was love. I was a child. I didn't know.

You are a child. Tess—

I heard you flush the toilet. I heard you go back to Mama and wake her up and shake the bed. I heard you leave in the morning, before it got light. I never told her, Blue. I waited for you to come back to me, and a few nights later you did.

I never touched you. I covered you up. I never went into your room again.

You came back, Blue. You came back again and again.

Tess—

You stood me up against the wall. You sucked my nipples. You pressed your fingers into me.

Tess, he says, but his voice is fading.

I thought it was love, I say. I wanted you to come back. I kept it hidden from Mama. It scared me. It hurt me to hide it from Mama. It hurt Mama. But I wanted you to be there with me. You scared me, but I wanted you. When you stopped coming I got confused. I was ashamed. And then I forgot. It was all I could do.

His beer is empty. His eyes are closed. I feel him holding on. As if he's willing himself deaf. As if he's counting to ten. As if when he opens his eyes I'll somehow be gone.

I thought it was love, I say again. But it was so unlike love you don't even know you were there.

You're the one who needs help, I say. You won't even tell Mama you saw me today, will you? You won't tell her I love her. You won't tell her I'm sorry. You won't tell her I'm okay.

You're not okay. Tess—

You're alone now, Blue. I don't want you anymore. When Mama doesn't want you either, that's when I'll go home. That's when she'll believe me and that's when I'll go back.

Tess—

Stop repeating my name. Stop hiding in Mama. Do you want to ask her why if she really believes you're innocent she hasn't told my father, she hasn't called the police? She hasn't, has she? She can't save you. Nobody's going to save you. Nobody loves you now. I was the one that loved you. I thought you were good. But you're not good. You're too helpless to be good. You've got to save yourself and you can't even do that.

I stand up to leave.

You'd better eat my sandwich, I say. I haven't touched it.

He doesn't answer. His back is stiff. His head is bowed.

Tess, he says, but he can't go on.

I will not pity you, I say.

Outside the rain comes down like ice. I run. The rain is a gift. Other people are running. My heart is pounding. I don't know if he'll try to follow me. I leap down the stairs to the subway and buy a token. I hear a train and run. Far down the platform a man starts to whistle. I watch him pace. The train is gone. There is no one on the platform but the whistling man and me. The melody is slow and lonely. I wait next to the stairs, ready to flee. Three girls come down giggling. They chatter, bending their heads together, talking Spanish and English back and forth and running when they hit the platform. I remember Rainy and Jane. I remember hours and days and nights, giddy and whispering. I remember the cemetery, the beech forest, secrets, singing in our tree. I see Spider when his name was Dylan come into the pizza place and wink at us and kick the cigarette machine yelling Shit! We watch him go up to the counter demanding a dollar in quarters when suddenly the guy who owns the place comes down from upstairs waving his arms and shouting at us lousy damn kids to get out of his restaurant, he knows that lowlife didn't put any dollar in that machine, we're all just lousy kids, and Dylan's shouting back he did too put money in it, and they go on shouting like that until the guy who owns the place takes four quarters out of his pocket and drops them in the coin slot, pulls a knob without looking, tosses Dylan a pack of Kools and shouts even louder, Now all you get out of here. You don't buy my food, you get outta my place—what do you think this is here, some kind of a sleazy joint? and we all pile out together laughing and cross the street to the meat rack and stand on the benches and smoke Dylan's Kools and drape our bodies around the base of the town's memorial to its dead and returned veterans of World War I. I see Rainy and Jane leaning out over the grass. I see their faces against the stone. I see the wind blowing their hair. I hear them laughing. I see their eyes in Katie Roberts' kitchen the day she read my cards. The man's whistling echoes up the subway tunnel, resonant and patient and full of sorrow. I want a train to come. I can't stop moving. Everything is out of my control.

Tim tells me he knows a painter who might have a job for me. He's kind of crazy, he says, but good to kids and dogs. He'll take you to a ballgame if he likes you. I ask is he crazy enough to give me a place to sleep? Tim laughs. I don't know, he says. Do you have a place tonight? Sure, I say, I bought a room off some junkies. I'm rich tonight, I tell him. Can you give me this painter's number? and I try it but no one's home. I put on three layers of clothes. I find a wool cap and scarf in Spider's shopping bag. I drink a cup of hot chocolate and rub baby oil into my skin. By the time I hit the sidewalk, the sky is dark with clouds and snow is beginning to fall. I get an uptown train at Bleecker Street. I'll change at Union Square and ride the L back and forth to Brooklyn and sleep through the night. The cap and scarf will hide my face. If they slip and show my age and some busybody or Guardian Angel or cop gets involved, I'll act innocent and dumb. God, my mother, I'll say, she'll be so worried. I'd better call her right now, I'll say. I can't believe I fell asleep. What time is it, anyhow? If they make me I'll call Tim. I'll pretend he's Mom's boyfriend. If they want to hear his voice I'll hand them the phone. I can talk my way out of anything. I get off the 6 with the crowd at Union Square. I go up the stairs and down. Almost on the Canarsie platform, I hear a violin. My eyes open. It's just a panhandling musician. But the music is beautiful. As shocking as sunlight. All around me everyone is listening. An old Polish woman with a head scarf and swollen ankles. A muscular guy in grease-stained coveralls embroidered *Anthony* in red. Crowds of kids in leather jackets and Sergio Valente jeans. Office workers and waitresses and Guardian Angels and cops and bland young men in suits. A Latina with brown-eyed children and shopping bags. Two handsome black guys with pencil-thin mustaches. A Chinese grandfather. Orange-haired punks and subway bums. Everyone is listening. I can see the music on their faces, in their eyes. When the train comes I can't get on it. I sit on the bench and listen to the violin. The second train that comes, I get up and walk around the stairway so the violinist can't see me. I don't want him to notice. I don't want him to see I have nowhere to go. I sit on the bottom step listening. Hours later the crowds thin out. The violinist stops playing. I watch him walk up the stairs with his battered violin case. I sit there a while longer. I don't want to spend the night on a train. I get up and leave the subway. I walk down Broadway. The snow falls fast, in big wet clumps. I stop beside the fence at Grace Church and look into the yard—buried in snow, white and unbroken and clean. Lights are on in the side buildings, gold through the curtains and glass. Snow falls blue through the beams of the spotlights. The spire stands up silver, blocking out the night. I stand a long time, looking, my hands closed around the black bars of the fence, the falling snow soaking through my mittens to the skin. The church is so beautiful I can't believe I've ever gone into it. At last I turn away. I wander. I stop in diners. I have money tonight. I drink hot chocolate. I walk and walk. Somewhere off Delancey Street I see lights on a red and yellow sign that says OLYMPUS COIN-OP. I see lights in the windows. I see two winos sleeping on a bench inside the glass and another sitting hunched up staring at a wino sleeping on the floor. Except for the solitary hunched-up man, they all look warm. I go in. There is room for me on the long bench where the cold man sits alone. I hesitate. Before I can move he grabs my wrist.

When the diapers are all neatly folded the fat woman lifts the pile and carries it as if she's heading for the door. She stops. She puts the diapers down on top of a washer. She opens her purse and comes toward us holding out her hand. Adam's fingers are tight, gripping my wrist. I'm sobbing. I'm afraid, I'm relieved. I don't know what I feel. Hungry, angry, lost, tired. Everything at once. I shake from inside. I don't know what's going on. Adam shakes too, his fingers and his hand around my wrist. We're not looking at the woman. We're looking at each other. She comes very close before we know she's there. Tengo mucho dinero, she says. I don't drink no more. She clutches her breast. Mi corazón, she says. Aquí, aquí. In her palm she offers us quarters. You take, she says. I don't need. I move closer to Adam. His whole body is shaking, not just his hand. I sit down beside him and stare at the woman. He doesn't let go of my wrist. No, he tells her. Even his voice shakes. No, he says. In Spanish he says words I can't understand. The woman smiles and throws up her hands, her shoulders rise and fall. She takes her quarters across the room and divides them up among the sleeping winos. She leaves them close to their faces, carefully stacked. She comes back to the yellow washing machine and her pile of clean diapers. She opens the machine and stuffs them in. She drops quarters into the slot. Water comes crashing against the glass. She turns and grins, as if water is the miracle. She laughs. She says, They keep this laundry open for me. You don't know me? Soy la madre del mundo. I keep the devils away. Verdad, she says. Es verdad. She nods and waddles to her corner in the back, humming her song. She drops out of sight behind the machines. Her song fades. I can't stop sobbing. Adam lets go of my wrist and puts his arm around my shoulder. We sit there huddled together shaking in the bright fluorescent light.

Tess, he says. He looks at me, baffled. Tears run out his eyes. Where did you come from? he says. Where's Holly?

I want to answer him but I don't know how to begin. I can't go far enough back. He looks at me a while and pulls me close to him again. I can't see his face.

You can't be here, he says. It isn't you. He squeezes my arm. I feel him smile. You're here, aren't you? he says. You're really here?

I nod against his shoulder. I listen to his heartbeat.

And you're really Tess?

I nod again. Yes, I say.

I'm sorry I scared you, he says. I scared you, didn't I?

I shrug. He feels every gesture I make. I feel his trembling.

Tell me what you're doing here, he says.

I can't, I say. Not yet.

Okay, he says. He holds me close to his heart. Together we watch the sleeping winos across the room.

Adam? I say after a while.

He squeezes my shoulder.

Why are you here? I say. Why are you trembling?

I'm here to watch those men, he says. I'm here to keep myself trembling.

I pull back to look at his face. Tears dribble down his cheeks. I don't think he knows they're there.

I don't understand, I say. Are you drunk too?

No, he says. Not anymore.

He points at the laundromat clock. There's no one to talk to at three in the morning, he says. So these guys will have to do.

195

I don't understand, I say.

I've got the shakes, he says. I have the sweats. I hurt. Things happen behind me. Until I took your hand you might have been the DTs. I can't sleep and I can't stop shaking and if I take my eyes off those guys for a minute I'll go looking for a drink.

He shrugs. He smiles at me. Well, maybe I won't, he says. But I'm crazy anyway. If I weren't still crazy I wouldn't be sitting here, would I?

I don't know, I say. I don't want him to stop talking. I don't want him to ask about me.

When I couldn't sleep tonight, he says, I came out walking. I told myself if I found some pissy shitty drunks, if I put some poor freezing pissy shitty drunks in front of my face and kept them there I'd remember I was one of them. I am one of them. I'd remember that last week and the week before and I don't know how many weeks before that, I was hiding in alleys drinking pints out of paper bags scared of my shadow and scared of my reflection and scared of my own hands. I'd remember that every night I was so drunk I couldn't stand up. I had money enough to buy a room to pass out in. That was the only difference between these guys and me. Somehow I always woke up in a bed. And then one day, three days ago—almost four, he says, looking out the window—I couldn't do it anymore. I don't know what happened. I just gave up. I knew where I had to go. I've known for years. I've known where to go all over the city, all over the world. I didn't even have to make a phone call. I just walked into one of those rooms.

I don't know why, he says. The tears run down his face.

He closes his eyes and squeezes the tears and wipes them away.

I'm getting better, he says. Even sitting here I'm getting better. He holds his hand out in front of himself and watches it shake.

It comes and goes, he says. He shrugs. So that's my story, he says. What about yours? Where'd you get the funny haircut?

No, I say. No story.

I'm glad you're here, Adam, I say. I'm glad you're getting better.

Thanks, he says. I'm glad you're here, too.

You won't forget this then, will you? I say. I mean there's no reason for you to forget this? You'll remember I was here?

He laughs. Of course I'll remember. I'm not sure I'll believe it.

Well I want you to believe it. I'll give you something so when I'm gone you'll believe it. It belongs to you anyway.

Don't go, he says. Where are you going?

Just getting into my pockets.

But where are you going?

It's yours anyway, I say. I hand him his letter to Mama.

He looks at it. He takes it out of the envelope and looks at the words.

Tess, he says. Tess, sit down here again. He pulls my head close. I hear his heart. He rubs my funny short hair.

What is it, Tess? Why are you here?

He waits for me to answer. I shake my head against his chest.

He looks at the letter in his hand. Where is she, Tess? he says. Tell me where she is.

Florida must know, I say. She's working for Florida again I think.

He sighs. He works the letter into one of his pockets and settles me inside his arm.

I'm glad you're here, Adam, I say again after a while.

Sitting here with you is like being home with Mama, I say. But I can't go home yet. You have to let me go.

You can go whenever you want, he says. I won't stop you.

He pushes me back to look at my face.

I didn't hold you to stop you, Tess. I just wanted to know you were real.

Oh, I'm real, I say.

Tears come into his eyes again.

Don't ask, I say. Mama will tell you. Let Mama tell you, Adam. Don't ask me to.

Okay, Tess, he says. It's okay. Lean on me again. Sleep. You're tired. When it gets light we'll go to breakfast. My treat, he says.

I want you to tell Mama I love her, Adam. Tell her I'm sorry. Tell her I'll come back. Tell her I'll come back soon.

She was happy with you, Adam, I say. For a little while, she really was happy.

I wake up when the diaper woman empties the washer and moves her load to a dryer. Adam is smoking a cigarette. One of the drunks has disappeared with all the quarters. The others are snoring. Outside, it's still night. It's still snowing. I close my eyes again and think about Mama. I know that people like Grandma, older people, people from another time, people who have lived another kind of life, people like my dad or like that woman who tried to help me in Port Authority, even people like Tim, people who've never been crazy and who've never been drunks or loved drunks and who've never had to run away from home would ask *but where was her mother while all this was going on? what kind of mother is this, with these lovers, this transient life?*—and I want them all to know what they don't understand, that even in her absence Mama is the real hero of my story. I want them to understand how Mama loves me, that she loves me like she wanted her father to love her, that she loves me like no man has ever loved her, like her mother never loved her either, no matter how much her mother thinks she does or has. Because Mama loves me freely. She loves me like she loves herself. I want them to understand, I want them to understand again. My story isn't my own yet. My story is still hers. If I walk every street she will find me. I'm the one she lives with, I'm the one she needs to find. I'm the one who's with her even when we're both alone. She will find me when she's ready. I'm not the one who's lost.

Adam's heart beats under my ear. The winos snore. The snow falls. The diaper woman hums.

I have to leave now, Adam, I say. It's time for me to go.

The door opens. A chubby young deaf-mute with reddish hair and good eyes comes in. I know him. He's a Jesus freak. I've seen him on the subway. He passes out leaflets. He nods thanks when anyone accepts. He doesn't thrust the leaflet on you. He holds it out, he offers it, he waits to see if you want to take it, he lets you decide. Seeing him now I think he must never sleep. He comes up to me and Adam. He holds out a leaflet. "As It Was In The Days Of Noah." Printed in turquoise. Adam accepts. I shake my head. I'll read his, I say. I point. The deaf-mute smiles. He walks over to the two sleeping men. He puts a leaflet down close to each of their faces. He goes to the back to the diaper woman, as if he knows she's there.

I have to go now, I say again.

No breakfast? Adam says.

No breakfast, I say. If I stay with you any longer I'll let you take me to Mama.

Then money for breakfast? he says. And my rabbit's foot?

I laugh.

This one's special, he says. It's not for luck, it's for joy.

He digs around in his pockets.

So you'll know I was real, he says. He smiles.

The rabbit's foot is purple. It dangles in front of my eyes.

Thanks, I say. Thank you, Adam, and before I can cry again I kiss his bristly cheek and go out the door with the deaf-mute boy. We walk along together in the night. When he sees a diner's lights on he stops and offers me the leaflet. I smile. I take it. He smiles. He nods thanks. He nods good-bye. He goes into the diner, looking for troubled souls.

Somewhere on the street a gun is fired, and I tell myself it's China Blue. Homeless men are sleeping on the subway grates. Steam rises around their bodies, melting the falling snow.

At Battery Park I stand against the rail and watch the clouds lift. It's dawn and the light is green. The snow is falling gently now. Gulls are in the air. The ferry glides away toward Staten Island. Mama is here—in the salt-wet sky and the ocean smell of seawater washing up the Hudson. Mama is all around me. I am home. I have always been home. Soon I will go home to her. But not today. Today I'm going to ride the ferry. I'm going to let it rock me and I'm going to sleep. When I wake up maybe I'll call Tim's friend the painter. Maybe I'll visit Solomon. Maybe I'll call Dylan's mother and ask her how to write to him and write him a letter even though there's no place yet for him to write me back. Maybe I'll look for Katie Roberts and find a way to help her. Maybe I'll lie in the sun and take out Adam's purple rab-bit's foot and wait for joy to come. Maybe I'll lie in the sun. Maybe when I wake up the snow will be gone. Maybe this is the last snow and April really is here now. The trees will bud and the nights will be warm and the grass will grow thick and green. All over the city the light will change. The foun-tains will come on. Musicians will play in the street. I will be my own story. I will go home to Mama. But I will not be like her. I will not be like any of them. I will not be unhappy. I will not be so unhappy. I'm coming back, Mama, I say. But not yet. She is standing in front of a mirror, wrapped in a wine-red towel. Her hair falls wet around her face. She leans close to the mirror. She plucks out a golden chin hair. I'm coming home, Mama, I say, and she turns her head toward my voice, over her left shoulder, as if she's just heard me calling from another room.

Acknowledgments

Work on *China Blue* was supported in part by fellowships, residencies, and grants from the National Endowment for the Arts, the Fine Arts Work Center in Provincetown, the New York Foundation for the Arts, Yaddo, and Centrum. Lines from Nijinsky quoted in "Earth Tides" are from *The Diary of Vaslav Nijinsky*, edited by Romola Nijinsky (Simon and Schuster, 1936). The line from Kierkegaard in "Earth Tides" is from *Concluding Unscientific Postscript*, translated by David F. Swenson and Walter Lowrie (Princeton University Press, 1941). Quoted passages in "Ground Zero" are from Emily Brontë's *Wuthering Heights*. Song lines in "Ground Zero" are from Brian Eno and David Byrne's "Help Me Somebody."